MW01592835

Amber Shades

LAURA LEIGH LESKOVAC

Printed by CreateSpace, an Amazon.com Company
CreateSpace, Charleston SC
www.CreateSpace.com/4716282

Amber Shades is a work of fiction. The characters, incidents, places
and dialogue are the product of the author's imagination and are
not to be construed as real. Any resemblance to actual events or
persons, living or dead, is entirely coincidental.

Printed in the United States of America.

ISBN:1497357705
ISBN-13:978-1497357709

*This book is dedicated to my beloved black lab, Storm,
who camped out by my side day & night
during the writing of this story
and who sadly left this world long before its publication.*

ACKNOWLEDGMENTS

I'd like to acknowledge and thank the following people:

~ My mom who checked in daily on my progress
twelve years ago and encouraged me to continue.
Thank you for the great time we had on my research trip
and for sharing the best pizza ever in Times Square!

~ My husband Josh who has always supported
my obsession with writing and who has loved me enough
to embrace the extremes of my personality.
Thank you for giving me the freedom to pursue this endeavor.

~ My dear friend Aaron who bravely volunteered
to read my book before anybody else and
who awakened a dream that lay dormant for so many years.
Thank you for your inspiration.

AMBER SHADES

CHAPTER ONE

This is where it gets a little fuzzy. I had been drinking an awful lot. I hardly even recognized myself anymore. I had become so distracted, so distant. I was losing it. Or rather, I had lost it. Where was I even going? It was dark and the rain pelted against the windshield. The wipers couldn't keep up. The radio was blaring. It was so loud, it was deafening. But I was extremely tired. I could barely keep my eyes open. I closed them, I think, just for a second. I remember swerving. Suddenly alert and sober, I concentrated on the road ahead of me. I must've dozed again. Then I hit something. A deer, I presume. The car was spinning out of control. Then it stopped. My head hit the steering wheel and my neck snapped back violently. Complete silence. A warm sensation came over me. I licked my lips. Salty. I was bleeding profusely and quickly slipping out of consciousness. It was the darkest dark I had ever known. I tried to open my eyes, but I couldn't wake up. My eyelids convulsed, my lashes fluttering like someone dreaming heavily. I heard voices, but I couldn't make out what they were saying. Perhaps I was imagining them. Perhaps I wasn't. What had happened? What had I done? Where was I? My thoughts were blurred, my mind foggy. But the memories were still intact and becoming clearer. I was home again.

*   *   *   *   *   *   *   *   *   *   *

The changing leaves were falling as our parting words crispened the cool autumn air.

"I don't understand why you have to go."

His voice was solemn, yet steady.

"Nor shall you, my dear friend. Just wish me luck."

We embraced and I planted an emotionless kiss on his forehead. Gabe and I had a rather peculiar, yet riveting relationship. The camaraderie between us was mutual, but I believed that he was in love with me and although I cared about him deeply, I didn't feel the same.

We had known each other for as long as I could remember. He was my closest friend and had stayed by my side through troubled times. It was Gabe who consoled me when I was nine and found my beloved cat Whiskers lying dead in the road. It was Gabe who carried my backpack to school after I broke my arm on the playground when I was twelve, and it was Gabe who saved me when I was sixteen and my prom date stood me up. It was Gabe who loved me when it seemed that I had nobody else.

He would've been the perfect boyfriend, but I was too afraid to lose him. Instead, he was my best friend. That way he could never leave me; that way I would never have to suffer the heartache my father still endured from my mother leaving him nearly fifteen years before. It pained me to see him so forlorn after all this time.

"A true love never dies," my father once told me. "Even if it walks out on you."

After high school, Gabe and I both ended up attending the same college. I didn't want to leave my father to go away to school, so I studied at the local university. After all, he only had me. As for Gabe, he began at Oakdale College in Vermont, but after his freshman year, he came home—back to Riverdale, Ohio.

"I missed you too much, JC," he said laughing and reached out to ruffle my hair.

He knew I hated that, and he usually did it to change the subject, so even though I had my suspicions as to why it didn't work out, I kept them to myself and we never discussed it further. I was happy to have him back. I missed him more than I thought I would, and besides, nobody else called me JC except Gabe. He started it when he found out my middle name was Clydesdale—yes, Clydesdale. Julia Clydesdale Baker. My father explained sadly that my mother wanted another horse, not a baby, so it was her way of coping with her unwanted pregnancy.

"My little Clydesdale," she would say as she patted her bulging belly. Dad said he thought it was cute at first, but when I was born her disappointment became full-fledged and caused a strain in their marriage. She left my father when I was just a little girl, forcing him to raise me alone.

My mother had been a beautiful woman. She was slender with long, brown hair and green eyes. Except for the scar on her forehead, she was flawless. I hoped I would look like her someday. She wasn't home much, though. She was free spirited, I once heard my father say. I remembered all her lavish parties. Oh how she loved hosting parties. More than anything. More than me. I was never allowed to attend because I was a kid, and she didn't like kids. To her, children were a nuisance and she had no room for any in her self-centered world.

Still, I loved her. She was my mom, even if Grandma Ruth and Grandpa Joe said she was nothing but a tramp.

The first time I heard the word I had no idea what it meant. The day I asked her was the day she left. It was a vivid final memory of my mother.

It was my seventh birthday and my grandmother was throwing a dinner party for me at the Riverdale Country Club. I was so excited. I had never been to the country club before! I had on a brand new yellow dress with white tights and shiny white dress shoes that clicked on the floor with every step I took. I felt so grown up. My mother was braiding my hair when I popped the question.

"Mommy, what's a tramp?" I innocently asked her.

"Julia, wherever did you hear such a word?" she asked, surprised at my inquiry.

"From Grandma. She told daddy that you're nothing but a tramp. Is that like in the *Lady and the Tramp*, mommy?"

She never answered me. She dropped the brush

and the bobby pins she'd been holding and stormed out of the room. The rest was a blur. I remember hearing my mother screaming and my father trying to calm her down. Then Grandma Ruth walked in. She and Grandpa Joe had just arrived to pick us up. I was out of their view, crouching on the steps, watching the whole scene. My mother marched toward my grandma angrily and put her hands on grandma's throat, choking her and yelling words I was never allowed to say. Grandpa Joe stepped in and pulled mom off of grandma while my father watched in horror. I ran to Grandma Ruth's side while she gasped for breath. My mother pointed at all of us saying that she hoped we all got what we deserved. I had no idea what that meant. I was trying to be so brave, trying so hard not to cry. My mother didn't like when people cried. She said it was a sign of weakness and she had no sympathy for them or for me. As much as I tried to fight them, the tears came. It only made her madder. Her face was red with fury and her eyes, her beautiful green eyes, were glaring with vehemence as she walked out the back door.

Grandma grasped her chest and collapsed. Grandpa called her name and shook her over and over again. I was in shock as Grandma Ruth's lips turned blue. I heard dad on the phone, his voice broken through muttered sobs, pleading for help.

She was already gone when they got there. A heart attack, the paramedic said.

"She never knew what hit her," we were told repeatedly, as if to console us. But she did. We all knew she did.

That was the last time I saw both of them alive, on my seventh birthday.

After finding out about Grandma Ruth's death, my mother moved to Europe. She never came to the funeral, never came home, never said goodbye. I doubt she ever felt guilty for what had happened. I don't think the woman had a guilty bone in her body. She wanted to start over, my dad explained. In Europe she found the life she always wanted --one with luxuries and without children. Without me. I planned to confront her someday and ask her why she didn't love me, but I never got the chance. She was killed in a skiing accident when I was fifteen.

I never really knew a mother's love. My mother had taught me that love leaves. Love leaves when you least expect it; love leaves when you need it the most.

My father was the one person I could count on. He loved me unconditionally. He selflessly gave up firefighting and instead took a job at the Riverdale Post Office. It was a good job and he enjoyed the people on his route, but it wasn't quite as exciting as running into a burning building. I overheard Grandpa Joe and dad discussing it late one night.

"You're losing your spark, John," Grandpa told him. "You were born a fireman, not some pansy in shorts going door to door with the mail."

"I just can't risk it," my father told his father. "She's already lost her mother. She doesn't need to lose me too."

My father was very protective of me. He knew his work with the fire department was dangerous and he loved me enough to give it up. I loved him even more for that.

His love carried me through the rest of my childhood and through my most formative years. His love, ever present but never suffocating, let me become independent, to dream and to achieve. And with a love like that, who could ever expect more?

After graduation, I started working at our hometown newspaper, *The Riverdale Press*. Gabe got his degree in teaching and got a job at our alma mater in the History department. He was a fantastic teacher and all of his students adored him. We had lunch together as often as we could and we would spend the weekends together canoeing down the river in his big green canoe.

We suspected that everyone assumed we were a couple, and in a way we were—a couple of great friends who enjoyed each other's company more than anyone else's. I often wondered if it was healthy, though. For Gabe, I mean. I really didn't have any interest in meeting men. The only men I needed were already in my life—a wonderful father, a sagacious grandfather and my forever friend Gabe. Expecting more would just be setting myself up for disappointment. But Gabe needed more, and sometimes he looked at me as though he would just tackle me and smother me with all the passion and desire his eyes revealed. The thought made me shudder. I loved Gabe, but not in *that* way. I needed him to be with me always, not to leave me. Isn't that what always happened?

Not that it wasn't tempting at times. Gabe was very good looking. Women seemed drawn to him and often turned their heads when he walked by. He had chocolate brown hair and gorgeous brown eyes. He was naturally tan and by the end of summer he had a healthy glow that lasted well into winter. He was tall with broad shoulders and long, masculine legs. Not skinny, shapeless legs, but muscular and strong. He was the perfect height to play basketball, which he did very well. He played all through college and was the university's star player. I faithfully cheered him on at every game, although I secretly never really cared much for the sport. Still, I couldn't help feeling so proud of him when he would score and the crowd would wildly clap and holler for my Gabe. After every game I'd meet him at Baily's Pub where the players went to celebrate a win or mourn a loss. The guys considered me one of the gang. "Gabe's girl," they all called me and Gabe would just wink at me and smile.

He had a few girlfriends on and off, but nothing serious. He'd tell me all about their dates, but eventually he stopped seeing each and every one.

"They can't all be so bad, Gabe," I'd tell him.

"No, but they're not you," he'd tease.

Aside from our friendly hugs and occasional harmless flirting, I was careful not to get too touchy with Gabe, fearing he would mistake it for something more. I never dated and he never asked why. It wasn't for lack of offers, he knew that, but he also knew how hard I was working toward my dream job. I think he would've been jealous if I did go out with someone, especially one of his teammates, several of whom never made a secret of wanting to take me out. They'd jokingly ask his permission to ask me on a date.

"You can't keep her all to yourself, Gabe, especially if she's not your girlfriend," I remember one of them saying. He'd respond in a fatherly manner: "Just make sure she's home before midnight."

The more they drank at Baily's, the louder their banter would become. I would just smile at their foolishness and dismiss it as drunken jest. I wasn't interested anyway. I was focused on myself and my ambitions. I couldn't stay in little 'ole Riverdale forever. I hoped to someday be writing for a large city newspaper—*The New York Times* was my dream.

I enjoyed my small town job as a reporter at Riverdale's only newspaper. Everybody has to start somewhere, I'd remind myself. And Riverdale was a nice place to live—small, but nice. The town's population was under five thousand. There were two grocery stores, a few fast food restaurants and a bowling alley, but not much more than that. The ice-skating rink had been closed down for years and the theater only showed two movies that had played several weeks earlier in larger out-of-town theaters. The nearest shopping plaza had only a card shop, a liquor store and an old K-mart.

What the town lacked in shopping convenience, it made up for in beauty. Riverdale Park was one of my favorite places. When we were younger, Gabe and I would ride our bikes there, walk on the nature trail or just sit on a bench alongside the river and ponder the decisions we were making for our futures. Even though it sometimes seemed it was only the two of us there, the park was always lively with a baseball game underway or a band playing at the old stone amphitheater or children running around at the playground.

When I was a little girl, my father used to take me to the park to play in the sandbox and to swing. The swings were my all-time favorite. I'd beg him to push me higher and higher.

There was also a larger park about ten miles from town that was popular for fishing and boating. Gabe and I once rented a motorboat for the afternoon on the day of our high school graduation. We found a picturesque island where we docked to check it out. It was then that my suspicions that Gabe was falling in love with me finally surfaced. We were walking around the small island picking wildflowers for Mrs. Jones when I felt him staring at me.

"Did anyone ever tell you how beautiful you are, Julia?" he asked.

I blushed and threw my hair behind my shoulder and vainly said, "Yes, I am quite the princess, you know," hoping to change his serious tone. We both laughed at my sarcasm, but it didn't quite work. He reached toward me and placed a flower behind my ear.

"Now you are," he said, gazing at me. I quickly averted my eyes, avoiding prolonged eye contact and suggested that we get going. Most girls would've drooled over the chance to have Gabriel Jones alone in the woods on a beautiful June afternoon. I suddenly wanted anything but. I didn't want Gabe to want me the way a man wants a woman. I didn't want Gabe to love me the way a husband loves his wife. I wanted Gabe to my friend—to be with me throughout my life and not to leave me.

Instead, I did just what my mother had done to my father and me. I left. I left the newspaper. I left Riverdale. I left Gabe.

CHAPTER TWO

When my editor came into work on Monday morning, he was whistling as he hastened toward my desk. "Good morning, Julia," he sang.

"My goodness, somebody had a great weekend," I grinned suspecting that he and his latest fling had done nothing more than stay in bed.

"Well that, too," he said with a sly smile. "But that's not why I'm so cheerful right now."

"Do I have to drag it out of you?" I asked.

He looked directly at me and smiled even wider.

"Julia, we made it!" We're outta here!" He looked

like a little boy on Christmas day, excited over his new toys.

"What are you talking about, Ross?" I was puzzled and excited. His mood was contagious.

"You and me, babe. You are looking at a new co-editor of *The New York Times*," he continued on breathlessly, not giving me a chance to congratulate him.

"And I am looking at their newest reporter!"

"Ross, that's wonderful. But what on earth are you talking about?" My eyes were wide with anticipation, but I was still confused.

"I was hired at *The Times* and well, I sent them some of your articles. You're ready, Julia. They want you! We start next Monday!"

"You've got to be kidding. *The New York Times*?! Ross, you're a saint!" I was jumping with enthusiasm and we quickly drew everyone else's attention as we hugged each other and practically danced our way out of the office.

I first met Ross Carter when I was in high school. He was a reporter at *The Riverdale Press* and I had come for a tour. It was then that I decided I wanted a career in journalism. While in college I did my internship there and Ross had become the News Editor, moving toward his ultimate dream to work in New York City. And now he had made it and he was taking me with him. I was so overwhelmed. I instantly felt queasy. I had only ever dreamed of working at *The Times* and if I ever did get the chance, I expected it would take at least twenty years. Suddenly my life had changed and I couldn't miss out on such a golden opportunity. I had to go. *Start spreading the news...* New York City, here I come!

It was September—the perfect month of the perfect year of my life. My father was just as excited for me as I was. Gabe was a different story. Though he knew how much it meant to me, he said he didn't expect my departure from Riverdale to come so soon. After all, I was just a rookie reporter, he pointed out. And he said he was worried about me, that the city would swallow me up. I think he was trying selfishly to scare me, but his efforts were in vain. That Saturday Gabe drove me to the Cleveland Hopkins International Airport. The trip was silent.

* * * * * * * * * * *

When I arrived at LaGuardia Airport it was like stepping into a whole new world. As part of our contract, *The Times* agreed to give us an advance to pay for hotel rooms for two weeks for Ross and myself so that we could each find a place to live. They had sent a driver to pick us up, who was now waiting for us holding a sign that said: *NY Times Employees*. It was strange and surreal and exhilarating.

Ross and I hardly spoke a word to each other on the way to the hotel. He was looking out his window and I was gawking out mine, both so awestruck by the hustle all around us.

There were no rules. Pedestrians didn't wait for traffic, traffic didn't wait for pedestrians. Horns were blaring, police motorcycles were zooming in and out of traffic and an ambulance was stuck behind us—its lights flashing and its siren barely audible, with nothing to do but sit still. There were no rules when it came to fashion either. The styles were off the wall. A woman with blue platform tennis shoes at least eight inches high and matching blue hair raced across the street. A shiver ran through me. Gone were the quiet, neatly-lined streets of Riverdale. Gone were the lazy afternoons sitting on the porch with Grandpa Joe sipping iced tea. Gone were the familiar sounds of the crickets and the occasional hoot of a night owl. Gone were the people I loved the most and the only place I ever called home.

We were driving up Broadway in Times Square when the electronic super signs came into sight, advertising everything from men's underwear to vodka. The storefronts were brilliantly splashed with bright neon lights. I stared in awe at the large television screen I had seen every night during the introduction of the late show I watched. I couldn't believe I was there.

When we pulled up in front of the Casablanca Hotel, I hesitated before getting out. The limousine had felt so safe and now I was surrounded by uncertainty. I was excited, but I couldn't help hear Gabe's words replaying in my mind. "Swallow you up, swallow you up, swallow you up..."

I hoped he wasn't right. I could do this. And though he didn't know it, Gabriel Jones gave me even more incentive to do so. I was strong and independent and yes, I could make it here. Without a doubt. *If I can make it there, I'd make it anywhere. It's up to you. New York, New York...* Cheesy, I know. Still, it played in my mind as if it were my mantra.

The hotel was beautiful. No expenses spared there. It was situated in the heart of the Theatre District, near the Fashion District and just steps away from the newspaper. The lobby oozed sophistication. It was meticulously decorated with unique tapestries, beautiful murals and a large crystal chandelier. The woman at the front desk didn't speak fluent English and she repeated herself more slowly when I didn't respond to what she was saying. Ross took over while

I watched. I was intimidated already. A bellhop pulled over a gold cart and loaded our bags onto it before leading us to our respective rooms.

I unpacked and stood in front of the window staring at the amazing view. I felt as if I were born for the city. A knock on the door shook me from my thoughts.

"How are you settling in, kid?" Ross asked.

"Come in, I'm done unpacking. What about you?"

"Yep, done. And I'm hungry. Want to get dinner?"

I grabbed my purse and we went to the hotel lounge. In addition to our advance, *The Times* gave us an allowance for traveling expenses—a far cry from *The Riverdale Press* where reporters had to supply their own notebooks and pens. Rick's Café was on the second floor. It was an elegant, yet relaxing setting complete with an ornate fireplace in the corner. There were TV's along a wall near the bar and there was an assortment of newspapers and books on randomly-placed coffee tables. Classical music filled the air. It was an eclectic atmosphere. I ordered the chicken cordon bleu and Ross had prime rib. We were served a small shot glass of complimentary wine that neither of us liked, but the meal was delicious and the cheesecake we ordered for dessert was to die for.

Ross had relatives on Long Island that he planned to visit for the weekend, so after dinner I was on my own. I was too curious to sit in my hotel room and I needed some new clothes, so I hailed a cab and went shopping at Macy's. I bought two suits and a black faux alligator-skin bag, which I thought would be perfect to conceal my notebook and recorder. It was getting late so I went back to the hotel and called it a night. Before I went to bed, I thought about calling Gabe. Normally he would've asked me to call him as soon as I arrived so he knew I made it safely, but he never asked me to this time. I knew he was upset, but he was being selfish. Stubbornly, I thought maybe I'd be better off not thinking about Gabriel Jones anyway.

Sunday was absolutely gorgeous. The weather forecast had called for afternoon rain showers, but the morning was only full of sunshine. Shortly after I woke up, I called my father and told him all about the hotel and my first shopping adventure in the city. I didn't want to waste the day staying indoors, so I walked to Central Park. By the time I got there, my feet were aching and I was sorry I hadn't taken a cab, but the park was worth it. It was incredible to find nature in a place that seemed none existed. Aside from the bikers, rollerbladers and homeless people, there were ducks and squirrels, lots of trees and even park benches. Looking at an empty bench, my heart sank.

Gabe was still on my mind, even though I was willing him not to be. I knew this place would be my only sanctuary from all the craziness of the city. I walked and walked, not realizing how large the park was. Activity was all around me. A woman walking six dogs smiled at me as I veered around her. A group of elderly men were playing chess at built-in stone tables and a mime stared at me with his painted face and motioned his hands as if he were trapped inside a box. I tossed a quarter into his upside-down hat that laid on the ground beside him and I slowly made my way out of the park just in time to catch a cab before the rain poured down with little warning.

"Where to, young lady?" The cab driver sounded either tired or annoyed.

"Oh, umm," I didn't want to go back to the hotel yet. It was only five o'clock, but I hadn't thought about what I wanted to do next.

"I ain't got all day, you know. Time is money," he said. He was definitely annoyed.

"Sorry, I just got here yesterday. Can you recommend somewhere good to eat?"

"It's New York City. There's thousands of places to eat. You can't pick one?" He was not at all friendly, so I just asked him to take me to the Casablanca.

He glanced at me several times in his rear-view mirror and swore at his broken windshield wiper before he spoke to me.

"So what's a pretty girl like you doing in the city all alone?"

I may have been accused of being naïve before, but I wasn't stupid. "I'm not alone. My fiancé is with me, but he had a business meeting today, so I'm on my own for dinner."

"A bizness meetin' on a Sunday?" he asked skeptically.

"Yes, it was the only day his clients had free."

"He some kinda lawyer or somethin'?"

"A *criminal* lawyer," I lied.

"Well, Hard Rock on West 57th is a favorite for you young people. That where you wanna go?"

"No, thank you. The Casablanca on West 43rd will be fine." I had gone to a Hard Rock Café in Cleveland with Gabe and a group of friends once after going to a concert. It was fun, but it wasn't a place to dine alone. Sitting there by myself didn't sound very appealing. The music is loud and the atmosphere too obnoxious for my mood. I'd rather just go to the secluded restaurant at the hotel.

"That's fourteen dollars," the driver said as he slid in behind a limousine in front of my hotel.

"Keep the change," I said as I handed him a twenty. I had a habit of giving generous tips and Gabe often chastised me about it. "If you saved all the money you over tip, you could take yourself on a nice vacation," he said on more than one occasion.

But we all had a job to do, and they never paid as much as they were worth—except maybe *The New York Times*! I laughed to myself. Here I was, at 24 years old, about to embark on a chance of a lifetime.. and the only thing I could think about was what to eat!

I took the elevator up to my room on the fifth floor and changed my clothes before heading down to the café. My message light was blinking, but I ignored it. I was too hungry.

Rick's was empty and the rain beat against the windows, but it suited my mood. I needed to relax and settle the butterflies that fluttered in my stomach every time I thought about the next morning.

"Just one or are you waiting for your husband?" My thoughts were suddenly interrupted. I glanced at the waiter, puzzled, then I laughed. He was the same waiter Ross and I had the night before.

"Did I miss something?" He asked cautiously.

"I'll be dining alone," I said amused. "And I don't have a husband." The thought of Ross as my husband was hysterical. Ross was gay. I supposed a stranger wouldn't pick up on it right away, but after you knew him, it was blatantly obvious.

"I thought, I mean you walked in here with him arm in arm and shared your dessert," he stammered shyly. Wow. He was presumptuous and very observant.

I held up my hand to cease his embarrassment. "It's fine, really. He's my boss, well my friend, he used to be my boss." I was caught up in trying to explain my relationship with Ross that I didn't notice him staring at me.

"I'd like to say I'm sorry, but I'd be lying if I did."

The shy waiter wasn't so shy after all. I blushed. I didn't know what to say.

"So what will it be?"

"I'd like the grilled chicken salad with French dressing if you have it and a glass of water, please." Even though I was starving, I wanted to eat light so I felt my best come morning.

"Your eyes are dangerously beautiful," he said and brushed my hand as he took my menu. I tried to ignore the electricity that seemed to come from nowhere.

After dinner I went to the bar and ordered a white Zinfandel. I thought it might take the edge off. I was getting nervous thinking about the day that lay ahead of me and part of me was missing Gabe. On warm Sunday nights we usually went to Henry's Place for ice cream. I wondered if he was there, ordering his double scoop of chocolate chip cookie dough. I wondered if he was thinking of me. I wondered if this would end up being the best thing for him. I was so deep into my own thoughts that I nearly fell off my stool when someone tapped my shoulder.

"Is this seat taken?" he asked.

It was the waiter and he looked really good in khakis and a deep orange polo shirt. A bit arrogant, not very original, but very good looking.

"Be my guest," I motioned toward the empty stool beside me, trying to seem uninterested.

"How's it going, Tom?" The bartender asked and poured him a drink without asking what he wanted. I pretended not to pay attention.

"I'm Tom," he turned to me. "And you are?"

"Leaving," I said. Without another word, I set down my empty glass, walked out the door and got on the elevator. The last thing I needed was the waiter from the restaurant. I was stressed enough. Tom. Ugh. What a dull name.

Ross met me in the hotel lobby at seven-thirty Monday morning. On the way to *The Times*, I was so nauseous with nerves. Was I really ready for this? Could I live up to their expectations or would my stay in the city end up just being a short vacation after all? Would the city "swallow me up?" I wondered if Ross was as nervous as I was. He looked so relaxed and calm, which made me feel worse. He had every right to walk through those doors—he had paid his dues in the business, working for years and years in the newsroom. He deserved this. I, on the other hand, basically was coasting in on his coattails. I had to prove myself here—Ross had already done that.

I met with my editor, Ed Garrison, promptly at eight a.m. He wasn't at all what I had pictured. He was a bit hard to look at if you know what I mean. He had gray hair and square-framed bifocals. I couldn't help but study the flaws of his face. His nose was grossly disproportional. In fact, I think it was the widest nose I had ever seen. And the pores on it were so large that it appeared to be speckled with polka dots. No, more like a strawberry. Yeah, that's what it reminded me of. But that wasn't all. There was a funny-looking raised mole on his left cheek that had two large black hairs growing from its center. His eyes were too close together and his eyebrows were wild and bushy. And his aura, the odor, was not very pleasant either. He literally reeked of garlic. I couldn't figure out what it was as first, but when I did, I was absolutely certain. It was definitely garlic and it seemed to ooze from his pores.

Perhaps I was being overly critical, but I guess I had imagined all of this for so long—and had glorified all of it. I had a vision in my mind that the city was going to be magical, like Oz, that the building would be the most impressive building I had ever walked into, that my editor would be the most debonair man I had ever met, that he would be polished and trendy, not overweight and dowdy.

Mr. Garrison gave me a thorough tour of the newsroom and showed me to my desk. I would meet the rest of the city-section staff at the daily ten o'clock editorial meeting. In all, there were more than a thousand employees in the news department. Ross had told me that the *Times* has the largest news staff of any newspaper in the country. But I won't be swallowed up. I refused to.

If I needed anything before the meeting, I was to see Connie, the veteran newsroom coordinator. My desk was already cluttered with office supplies and writing essentials. I still had an hour before the meeting so I sat down in *my* chair at *my* desk at *my* job at *The New York Times*!

I was so elated I felt as if I floated through the newsroom on the way to the conference room. That was until I bumped into another reporter and the stack of file folders she was carrying came crashing to the floor, scattering loose papers all around. Back to reality. I apologized profusely and tried to help clean up the mess I had caused. She looked very perturbed at first, but then she started laughing. I was relieved but still embarrassed.

"Don't worry about it. I did the same thing on my first day here, too, only I ran into Mr. Garrison and knocked his coffee out of his hand. It was a sight. His mug fell, and the coffee spilled into his briefcase and splashed onto his pants and onto his shoes, and my goodness, you'd have thought I did it on purpose. He looked at me with such anger that I burst into tears and ran to the ladies room, only before I got there I tripped over the leg of a chair and fell right on my face and tore my pantyhose and cut my knee. I thought about running out and never coming back, but I knew I'd never get a chance like this again, I mean I couldn't even believe they hired me in the first place. And here I am, three years later."

She finally took a breath.

"I'm Anna. What's your name?"

She was the most high strung person I had ever met. I couldn't imagine her interviewing anybody. And her articles must be more like short stories, the way she goes on and on and on. But she was friendly and I would definitely need an ally to help me learn the ropes.

"Nice to meet you, Anna. I'm Julia. And I'm glad you didn't have a cup of coffee in your hand!"

She laughed at that and by the time we got to the meeting I already had the scoop on the staff I'd be working with and I knew all about Anna's ex-husband

and his mother and his new girlfriend. But at least I had made a friend.

After the meeting, Mr. Garrison met with me to give me my initial assignments. Then I had the rest of the day to get settled in. For the next two days, I was supposed to become familiar with the city. There were twenty-two police precincts just in Manhattan alone. Talk about overwhelming. Riverdale had a small police department with only a handful of officers that everybody knew by name. The chief was a local celebrity in a way. He always led each of our holiday parades, attended the local town hall meetings and loved having his picture in the paper. One look at the map of lower Manhattan quickly reminded me that I was a world away from home.

I wasn't assigned to a "beat" yet. Most reporters are given a beat, which is a particular area or organization they report on regularly. It's easier for a reporter rather than chasing after a story in an unfamiliar area of the city and the reporter has the advantage of having a contact person. Ross taught me about beats during my internship. I remember him saying they are beneficial for both parties because a relationship can be built between the two that would provide the paper with information and updates. Plus, the contact is more trusting and apt to cooperate so that the story will be printed without errors or misunderstandings.

We didn't have beats at *The Riverdale Press*. We only had three reporters who covered all the town's news depending on who was where. This would be totally new to me.

Thursday and Friday were scratched off my work calendar for apartment hunting. Even looking at the calendar was overwhelming! How would I ever find a place in just two days? I took a deep breath and assured myself that I'd be okay, that I wouldn't get swallowed up, even though Gabe's words were haunting me already. *You can do this, Julia,* my inner voice was cheering me on. *Gabe is wrong. You got this.* I sure hoped she was right. And at least I had some help. Connie, the newsroom coordinator, had made the arrangements and she paid great attention to details, according to Mr. Garrison.

"I'm sure she has thought of everything you need help with, Ms. Baker," he said. "So meet with her for your itinerary."

I returned to the hotel after my first mentally exhausting day of work and was surprised to find a beautiful vase filled with yellow roses sitting on the desk in my suite. Yellow roses—my favorite. I was even more surprised when I read the card.

> *"Hope your first day went well.*
> *-- Tom"*

Tom? The waiter? I was certain they were from Gabe or my father, but Tom? How did he know about my job? He must've been listening to my dinner conversation with Ross. I was a little giddy over the idea of a romantic fling with Tom, but I was suddenly uneasy, concerned about how the flowers got into my room. I called the front desk and the attendant assured me that it was customary for the concierge to deliver flowers and other packages to the suites.

"You can rest easy, Ms. Baker. No staff has access to the rooms," he said in a casual tone. "Our guests usually find it refreshing to be greeted by a bouquet or gift rather than having to pick it up down here."

I agreed and thanked him, but I didn't apologize for being cautious. I had heard many horror stories about the city and I was determined to not let my guard down, especially so soon. But what really scared me the most of all were my thoughts of Tom. He was seriously handsome with his blond hair and mischievous blue eyes. I wondered why he worked at Rick's. He should be in magazines, I thought. I knew I should stay as far away from him as possible, but I couldn't help being tempted to once again dine in the café.

The day had been fairly warm but breezy, so I put on my short-sleeved burnt orange wool sweater and a long brown skirt with high brown leather boots. I loved the fall—not only for the weather, but also for the colors. Autumn shades best accented my skin tone, for I was often told that my favorite bronze lipstick and earth-brown eye shadow were perfect for my complexion. I looked in the mirror a final time and was pleased with my reflection. I ran my fingers through my long brown hair and headed for dinner.

I was disappointed to discover that Tom had the night off, so I quickly ate a Neptune Salad. Gabe ordered it once at Riverdale's Country Club and it became one of my favorite meals—light and refreshing. When the server set it down in front of me, I smiled at its familiarity—a plate of fresh fruit that surrounded a scoop of crab salad. Then I went to the bar for a Cape Cod. I deserved it, I rationalized to myself. After all, I did have a stressful day. I was halfway done with my drink when Tom strolled in and sat next to me.

"I knew you'd be back," he said smiling.

"I wanted to thank you for the flowers. That was really sweet but totally unnecessary." I was trying to play it cool, but dang did he look hot.

"Well that's why I sent them. If we only lived a life of necessity, we wouldn't be sitting here enjoying these fine drinks, now would we," he asked rhetorically. "I never did get your first name though."

That's right. I never did tell him. How did he know what room to have the flowers delivered to then? I thought about this for a nanosecond before I concluded that he must have had someone watch me return to my room. It was borderline creepy. He wouldn't have known from the registration. I always booked rooms under J. Baker when I traveled alone— for safety. But my gut told me he was safe.

"It's Julia," I extended my hand to his. I felt I owed him at least that much.

"Pleased to officially meet you, Julia," he said and kissed my hand.

My breath caught in my throat.

"What do you say we get outta here and take a walk? It's a beautiful night."

The bartender interrupted to ask if we'd like another drink and out of the corner of my eye, I saw him wink at Tom. They exchanged a knowing smile and I immediately felt sick with suspicion.

"So this is your game," I blurted.

He looked puzzled.

"Am I your latest bet? This week's challenge? First flowers, then what? Do you think I'm a fool?" I fired the questions at him without giving him a chance to answer. Then I got up and walked toward the door.

"Julia, wait!" he yelled. "Please, I'm sorry." He caught up to me and grabbed my arm. I spun around, staring straight into his eyes.

"It's not like that. I, it's just that, well the bartender thinks you're beautiful and that you'd never come back to the bar and I guess he was pleased to see you sitting next to me," he explained. His eyes were searching mine, but I only stared blankly and then sighed.

"I'm sorry," I apologized. "It's just that I don't trust many people and it seemed as though…"

I stopped mid-sentence and stared at the floor.

"I know how it probably looked, but I honestly didn't mean anything by it. Maybe some other time, okay?"

I thought about it for a split second.

"Do over?" I asked and he raised an eyebrow. I quickly extended my hand.

"I'm Julia."

He laughed and shook my hand. "They call me Tom."

"So Tom, how about that walk?"

We walked for at least an hour before we went back to the hotel. The city's buildings were silhouetted against the bright skyline and I shivered realizing that I was actually there—New York City. It still hadn't sunk in. Neither had missing Gabe or my father. None of that bothered me on this night. Everything was so new and exciting. And Tom was such a mystery. We talked about our lives, basically our likes and dislikes, our pasts and our present. He was so easy to talk to and he was a great listener too. I immediately liked him, but there was something about him that I was unsure of. I dismissed it as my usual skepticism.

Tom told me he was working at the hotel while he looked for the job he really wanted. He had an acting degree from Columbia University. He said he had loved the theater as long as he could remember and he worked at a nearby playhouse on weekends. He was hoping to get his big break in daytime television.

"You really want to be a soap star with all that drama?" I asked incredulously.

He laughed. "It's not like it's real drama. And I know it's a longshot, but it's what I see myself doing. Who knows though, maybe I'll end up working at Casablanca the rest of my life," he sighed.

"No you won't. You'll get there." Although we had just met, I could tell Tom wasn't the type to settle.

"Oh you know me so well, Miss Julia," he teased.

It was after ten when we got onto the elevator together. Tom pressed the button for the third floor and I leaned over him and pressed the five. It was an awkward silence as the elevator crept up three floors and came to a halt. The evening had been so pleasant, I didn't want it to end. I don't think Tom did either, but would it be too forward to ask him to my room? I didn't want to give him the wrong impression. I wasn't *that* kind of girl. I did enjoy his company, though, and I was lonely. As the doors opened, I saw my chance narrowing.

"Tom, um," I stammered before my confidence took over. "Would you like to come up and join me for a cup of tea?"

"No thanks," he said and I felt a sinking feeling inside. He smiled at my obvious disappointment. "To the tea, that is. I'd love to continue our conversation."

So that was that. Tom and I sat on the sofa in my suite and watched a movie until my yawning got the best of me and I fell asleep before it ended. I woke up at three a.m., surprised to find the TV off and a blanket draped over me. There was a note from Tom on the table.

*"Julia, you looked too peaceful to disturb, so I
saw myself out. Thanks for a great evening.
~ Tom"*

After a tedious second day meeting various contacts around the city, I drew a warm bath and soaked in an herbal bath salt—refreshing for mind, body and soul. At least that's what the label on the curvy glass bottle claimed. Connie from *The Times* had arranged an appointment with a realtor on Thursday of that first week and I had no assignment for Friday. They wanted to break me in slowly, my editor said. So I had only one more day before a long five-day weekend. Anna said she heard they were switching my position and didn't want me to start yet, so this was an intentional delay.

Either way, I had no choice in the matter, so I was going to be in NYC for five days and had nobody to spend it with—except for maybe Tom, I quickly reminded myself, and my thoughts of work suddenly transformed to thoughts of him. While in my robe, I sat on the edge of the bed and stared at the phone for at least an hour wanting to call him but afraid that it was too soon. I struggled against the urge to just pick up the damn receiver, and just when I was about to succumb, the phone rang. The jolt startled me so much that I nearly fell off the bed. I instantly regrouped and grabbed the phone. It was Tom. I played mind games with myself for several seconds before I said hello. I answered too soon, sounded too eager, as if I were waiting all night for the phone to ring. *You're pathetic*, my inner self told me. *He's gonna think you're desperate and that's a turn off.* I was beginning to scare myself. Why did I care so much about what this Tom guy thought anyway?

When the phone call ended, I smiled at myself in the mirror. I never let myself get so excited over a man before. I laughed at my girlish giddiness. So far New York had given me more than I bargained for. Tom asked me to meet him Friday afternoon at a bistro in Soho. He seemed excited when I told him I had a few days off before really starting my job, but he didn't say much about it—just to meet him at two o'clock.

The next day was torture. All I could think about was Tom. I met Anna for lunch at *our* place. I had only known her for a week, but it seemed like we had been friends forever. We had already claimed the Times Square Delicatessen as our regular lunch hangout. It wasn't anything fancy—basically just a pizza parlor. A pizza parlor with the best pepperoni pizza I have ever tasted, mind you. The place was small, but cozy and only a few doors up from *The Times*. One wall was covered with mirrors, so it appeared much larger than it actually was. I felt at ease with Anna, but I was disturbed over the way one of the servers stared at me incessantly. She was Spanish, no maybe Puerto Rican, and she had a long braid of black hair that went almost to the middle of her back. Every time I glanced in the mirror, I would catch her looking our direction. At first, I thought maybe she was amused by the way I was eating. Anna just laughed as I reached for yet another napkin. I struggled to hold my slice of pizza while I contemplated telling her about Tom. No wonder the woman was staring. Geez. Another napkin, please. Trying to prevent the grease from running down my hand was an art.

"Only a true New Yorker knows how to eat it right," Anna said, and showed me how to strategically place my finger in the center of the crust, causing my slice to fold together, creating a gully for the oil to run through. I thought I was doing pretty well, but the woman was still watching me.

Anna rambled about her ex-husband and the nerve he had flaunting his pregnant girlfriend in front of her when she saw them at her favorite restaurant.

"He knows Santos' is *my* place. Why on earth would he ever take *her* there? I mean, who does that?" she asked.

"I don't know, he sounds like a real creep," I said. "Does it bother you to see him with someone else? Why did you get divorced anyway?" I didn't want to pry, but I needed to understand her better. All she had told me about was how they had met, when they split up and I think she threw in how annoying some of his habits had become. I particularly remembered that she said he would clean out his ear with the end of his fork while he was eating. I was repulsed by him and had never even met him.

"God girl, didn't I tell you?"

"Tell me what?" I asked between bites.

"That son of a bitch got Miss Blondie pregnant while we were still married," she said matter-of-factly.

"Oh Anna, I'm so sorry. I had no idea."

"We've only been divorced for six months. I filed the day he told me about what's-her-name. I didn't even think twice. I heard affair and baby, and I headed straight to an attorney. I think I was in denial at first, or too mad to be upset, but I broke down a month later—on our fifth wedding anniversary—and couldn't stop crying for days. I told Ed I was sick and I took two weeks off. Vacation, I said, but I think he knew. I mean, the first thing I did when I went back was throw away all the pictures I had of him on my desk."

Anna looked so lost in her own thoughts for a moment as she stared down at her plate and concentrated on the orangey stain her pizza had left. When she looked up, I saw tears in the corners of her eyes, but she smiled and said, "Enough about me. What are you doing this weekend?"

I thought it would be too tacky to mention Tom now, but I had only one friend in New York and that friend was Anna.

"I met someone a few nights ago," I said cautiously, trying to hide my goofy grin.

"Do tell," she urged me to continue.

"I just don't know if I should get involved with him. He's just too irresistible." I told her all about the flowers and the walk we took and how he covered me up and left me sleeping.

"Sounds like a dreamboat. I'd go for it! There's nothing worse than a reporter without a story of her own," she said. "Emotion provokes writing—good writing, anyhow."

Anna was a gem, for sure. She was full of knowledge, yet she looked like a scatterbrain with her oversized glasses and her hair haphazardly twisted up with a pencil. She described herself as a curmudgeon—a cantankerous person who liked to quarrel with others for the sake of making a point.

"Curmudgeons are the people who return the oven cleaner that doesn't clean for the money-back guarantee," she explained when I looked confused. "You know our kind," she continued. "We trot back to the grocery store, receipt in hand, to point out we were charged full price for the spaghetti sauce that was on sale." She said she hadn't known there was actually a term for her crazy ways until she read a magazine article while waiting at her dentist's office.

"You should be grateful there are people like us," she said. "After all, we fight for you, for the principle—even if it means spending an hour on the phone to get back a dime."

I told her that sounded ridiculous and she just laughed. It was refreshing to have a girlfriend to joke with and not worry about offending. I never really had many friends. I didn't enjoy the usual female gossiping and cliques, and thus far I had been successful at avoiding as much girly drama as possible. But Anna was different. She and I were on the same wavelength from the beginning. She was a keeper.

Aside from her eccentricities, Anna was full of pain, yet she still wore a contagious smile. I would later find out that she and her ex had been trying to conceive for two years without success. She was convinced it was he who had the problem until her worst fears were realized with the announcement of his baby on the way. He, like Tom, had also been a waiter before they got married, but according to Anna he hadn't been able to hold a steady job since then. She loved him, though and her salary was enough to support his frequent unemployment and her frugal lifestyle. Anna admitted that he had never been her "knight in shining armor." No romance, no flowers. And sex with him had never been extraordinary, she said. She said she thought their love life lacked excitement, but she chalked that up to a heavy workload and the toll of marriage. She read somewhere that sex fizzles after marriage like a Fourth of July sparkler slowly meeting its demise. And that was okay with her, at least that's what she said. Apparently it was not okay with him.

Waiting for Friday seemed like waiting for an eternity, although I kept myself busy. The realtor was proficient. She knew what I was looking for and she didn't waste any time. After looking at a half dozen apartments, I finally found one that I could afford and could call home. I was excited to move in. It was my first place of my own. I could already imagine what I wanted and where. I planned to tell Tom all about it at lunch, but when I arrived at the restaurant, I didn't see him anywhere. After waiting ten minutes, I suddenly began to feel foolish. Perhaps he stood me up. I was angry with myself. Why did I let him to get to me like this? Why did I ignore my instincts? And dang it, I had looked forward to seeing him all week despite the taunting from my inner self who was telling me to stop thinking about him, telling me it wasn't a good idea, telling me I should concentrate on my new job and not on Mr. Charming. I was just about to leave when the waitress came to my table holding a small card.

"Are you Julia?" she asked.

"Yes," I answered.

"Then this is for you."

I opened the tiny envelope that had my name scribbled on it in Tom's writing.

"Julia,

Hope you don't mind eating solo, but I had a few loose ends to tie up. Your presence is requested at Casablan-

*ca's lobby at precisely 6:30p.m. Please pack a bag for the
weekend if you care to spend it with me.*

Yours, Tom"

I was re-reading the note, half amused with a
crooked smile, when the waitress brought me a plate
of fresh greens covered with grilled squash and zuc-
chini and drenched in a vinaigrette dressing.

"I haven't ordered yet," I interjected even though
the food smelled delicious.

"This was ordered for you, ma'am," the woman
said.

Was Tom for real? I was impressed. Not only was
he gorgeous and charming... *yes, inner self, you are
right that he is charming...* he was thoughtful and already had a good feel for my taste. A little too bold for
my comfort, but definitely exciting. I ate quickly.
There was so much I needed to do to get ready. I had
no idea what to pack, but I figured some new clothes
couldn't hurt, so I left hurriedly and went shopping.
My final stop was at a perfume counter where I was a
bit overwhelmed by all the fragrances. I chose a light
distinctive scent that evoked romance, according to
the sales lady. Yikes, it was expensive. I didn't usually
wear perfume, especially those with price tags over
$100 a bottle, but I also didn't go away for the week-
end with men I had just met, so I guess there's a first

time for everything.

I wanted to call Anna and tell her about Tom's surprise, but my inner self told me not to. *She'll say this is a bad idea. She'll tell you it's too soon. She'll tell you not to go.* Ugh, damn inner voice. She was relentless. Go away. I'm going and nobody is stopping me, I told her. Not even you.

I met Tom in the lobby with a suitcase in hand and he kissed me hello.

"You smell delicious," he said as he took my arm in his and led me to a car parked at the curb.

"Is this yours?" I asked him, surprised that he could afford a Spyder on a waiter's salary.

"I'm full of surprises," he said with a wink.

I slid into the soft leather seat. He turned on the radio and put his hand on my knee as he drove us out of the city and into a weekend of bliss. I had no idea where we were headed and I didn't care. All I could think about was the black negligee that I had brought along as I watched him shifting gears in the sporty car. There's just something about a man shifting that turns me on. Not really sure why, but oooh la la. Maybe it was the way the veins on his hands intensified. Maybe it was the way his fingers clutched the stick so firmly, holding steadfast as it shook and easing up only to jerk it in and out of gear. It's just so masculine. So hot. Oh, so hot.

A few hours later we pulled up in front of a breathtakingly beautiful bed and breakfast in Connecticut. It was dark, but the moon shone over the grounds illuminating a small creek with a bridge over it, leading to what looked like stables. Tom put his arm around me as I gazed at the stars.

"I could think of nothing I'd rather do than go riding with a pretty country girl like you" he said quietly. Then he held my chin firmly as he planted a kiss on my forehead, then my nose, then my mouth.

My tongue tangled with his as we stood there in the moonlight. Our passion for each other didn't stop there. Once inside our room, we no sooner dropped our bags to the floor when we locked lips and fervidly searched each other's eyes, trying to determine if this was too fast too soon. I undid the top button of his shirt and he pulled me closer. He kissed my neck and nibbled on my ears until I had his shirt off, then he lifted my arms and pulled my shirt over my head. We fell to the bed where we rolled over and over, one on top of the other, before he finally unzipped my skirt. I reached in the darkness for the bulge in his pants and cupped it in my hand before freeing him of his pants. He unsnapped my bra with his teeth and literally tore my panties off my body with an urgency that frightened, yet excited me. He spread my legs wide and plunged himself into me, pumping in and out with a fiery desire. His passion exploded inside of me, sending hot surges through my body. Without a word, he lit a cigarette and walked to the window, naked and still fully erect. I sat up and wiped his sweat off my chest, my head still spinning from the speed at which everything happened. It certainly wasn't the way I pictured our first night together, but I couldn't complain either. Tom lived life in the fast lane and I guess that didn't stop with me.

Still silent, Tom turned from the window and headed toward the bathroom.

"Coming, Julia?" he beckoned.

Trancelike, I followed him into the shower. The cool water trickled down my body, exciting my nipples and Tom stood behind me, his erection pressing into my backside He spun me around and kissed me hard on the lips before he demanded that I get to my knees. Nobody had ever talked to me like that before, commanding sexual pleasure. Stunned, I obeyed.

"Suck it hard," he ordered and I did, swallowing him whole while he held onto my head by my hair, forcing me up and down. When he was done, he got out of the shower, dried off and sauntered back to the bed. I looked in the mirror, wondering who I had become. A sex slave to a man I barely knew, that's who. But instead of being disgusted, I was aroused by this side of myself I never knew existed. I liked sex, and on this night it wouldn't have mattered if he had been a complete stranger. I wasn't in love with Tom, at least not yet anyway, and we didn't make love—we had sex. Straight, adult, pleasurable sex. And I could play this game too. I blew myself a kiss in the mirror and walked out of the bathroom a different woman—one who knew what she wanted and had just as much control over her life as Tom had over his. I climbed onto the bed and stood over Tom's surprised face and sat down, burying his nose in my crotch. I writhed around for a while as he obliged me, then I got down and laid beside him.

"Good night, Tom," I said dreamily. I think the cat got his tongue.

The next morning we ate breakfast, then went horseback riding. There were miles of trails and since I was an experienced rider, we didn't need a guide. The fall leaves were beautiful with their majestic hues of red, orange and gold. Free from the trees, they circled above me dancing in the wind. My horse stopped to drink from the stream as it trickled by. What a perfect place. I sighed, content with my surroundings but uneasy about the previous night's rendezvous. Tom's confidence made me feel like a different woman— bold, but cheap. I only had time to contemplate our relationship for a moment before Tom hopped off his horse and tied the black stallion to a tree.

"Let's take a break here," he said. Within seconds we were rolling around on the ground, just a few steps back from the well-worn path. The thought of being seen never occurred to me. We were alone in the world as far as I was concerned. Just Tom and Julia and two bewildered horses.

He pinned me down on the grass, his legs straddled over my body. He kissed my neck all the way down to my cleavage and bit my nipple through my thin t-shirt. Ahhh. It hurt, but it felt so good. He held both of my arms over my head with one hand—a very strong masculine hand. With his other hand, he unbuttoned and unzipped my jeans and slid it under my panties. He brushed his hand over my pubic hair before slipping a finger inside of me to make sure I was ready for him. I moaned with pleasure and squirmed underneath him. I wanted him. Badly. Now. I lifted myself up from the ground just enough to get my pants down over my backside and I reached down impatiently and fumbled with his button. He yanked my pants off the rest of the way and stood up quickly to rid himself of his own restricting jeans. He lowered himself over me and with one swift move, he lifted my leg onto his shoulder and thrust himself deep inside. He slammed into me repeatedly, faster and faster. I trembled beneath him and we climaxed simultaneously. Damn, he was a good lover.

After dinner, Tom had strawberries and a bottle of champagne delivered to our room. Feeling alive and wanted, I retreated to the bathroom for almost an hour as I doused myself in perfume and put on the black nightie I had gotten for what I thought would be our first time together. Of course, I had no idea the weekend would turn out the way it did, but it had been exhilarating and I didn't want it to end. When I opened the door, I had a sly sexy smirk on my face and expected to see Tom lying in bed. Instead, he was gone. I opened the room door and peeked into the hallway, but no Tom. Flashing lights caught my attention and I pulled back the curtain from the second-story window to look down at Tom talking to a police officer. I opened the window, straining to hear their voices, but I couldn't make out what they were saying. The officer was pointing to Tom's car. Tom shrugged his shoulders and handed over what looked like a piece of paper. A couple minutes later, they shook hands and the officer got back in his cruiser and drove away. I stepped back from the window and waited for him.

"Is something wrong?" I asked him when he walked in. He looked perturbed.

"No. Everything's fine," he said, but his eyebrows were furrowed and he was clenching his jaw.

"Then why were the police here to see you?" The reporter in me always needs to know the whole story, not half-truths.

"There was just a mix-up. That's all," he explained. "Let's just forget it, okay? Besides, you look too damn gorgeous to let this nonsense interrupt our weekend."

My negligee wasn't on for long. The night was incredible and endless. I was exhausted on the way back to the city, but the butterflies in my stomach wouldn't let me rest. There were such exciting, new feelings fluttering around inside of me and I couldn't wait to tell Anna about my unbelievable weekend.

CHAPTER THREE

Gabe finally called in mid-October. We talked like old times and I realized just then how much I had missed him. I didn't mention Tom, though. In some odd way I felt like I had betrayed Gabe.

According to him, nothing new was happening in his life. His students were lining up dates for Riverdale's homecoming dance after the last home football game. I hadn't missed one since I graduated. Ever since Gabe started teaching, I had accompanied him to the yearly dance, not as his date but as a fellow chaperone. I was laughing at his classroom anecdotes when I suddenly felt my first pang of homesickness.

How I longed to be sitting next to Gabe on my father's old porch swing, sipping apple cider and deciding what we'd be for Halloween. What he said next surprised me.

"I'm gonna be in the Big Apple the first week of November," he said. "I had hoped that maybe we could get together and you could show me your place."

I was speechless. I glanced around the room to see Tom's khakis and silky red boxers strewn about. Should I tell him another time would be better? I wanted to see him, but so much had changed in my life since we last saw each other. I had even cut my hair shorter—at Tom's insistence, of course. He said I would look more professional with a trendy above-the-shoulder hairstyle. Gabe had always loved my long hair and grimaced when I'd toss around the idea of getting it cut. "Not my Julia," he had said. "She'd never cut her hair." Oh, but she did. That was then and this was now and my life in New York was a world away from my life in Riverdale. It frightened me to think of letting Gabe see the new me and most of all, to introduce him to Tom. I wanted to keep that part of my life separate from this one—I was no longer the girl who feared relationships, who fled from commitment, who was happy alone.

His voice brought tears to my eyes. I couldn't lie to Gabe. "That would be wonderful," I told him and gave him the address.

The next time I talked to him was when he called from a cab to tell me he was only a few blocks away. I had been restless all day in anticipation of his arrival. I was eager to see him, but was uneasy about our reunion. I know it had only been a couple months, but it seemed like a lifetime ago that I left the little town of Riverdale.

I hadn't decided if I was going to tell him about Tom. Tom had been sleeping over at least twice a week, but this weekend he would be in New Jersey visiting his sister. I had already rid the apartment of any trace of him, carefully hiding his toothbrush and his blue-striped Oxford that I usually wore to bed. I felt a bit guilty doing it, but I just wasn't ready. I didn't want to spend the whole weekend seeking Gabe's approval of Tom. God knows he would have hated him anyway. He would have smirked at the prospect of Tom becoming an actor. "Promising," I could hear him say in his condescending way. Besides, Gabe would only be in New York one night and we had enough to catch up on without arguing over Tom.

When he pressed the buzzer, my heart nearly leapt out of my chest. I had been a nervous wreck all day. A flood of feelings I had put aside all poured out when I saw him. He put his arms around me, lifted me up and kissed me on the cheek before putting me down.

"JC, you look great," he said.

"What about my hair?" I asked him.

"Even your hair," he said as he removed his gloves and unbuttoned his long winter coat.

"Oh Gabe," I hugged him for at least thirty seconds. He felt so good, so familiar, so home.

We went to dinner at an upscale seafood restaurant where Gabe ordered the Orange Roughie and I ate Coquille Saint Jacques, my favorite. Then we walked back to my place, taking a slight detour through Central Park. Winter in New York City had thus far been brisk, not yet bitter cold, but it had begun snowing while we were finishing our dinner and now I wished I'd worn my scarf.

Gabe looked handsome, as always, clad in a gray J. Crew cable-knit sweater and black dress pants. Over our meal I learned that he was in the city to meet his Great Aunt Faith's attorney. She had died nearly a month before and left him executor of her will, even though he hadn't seen her in years. She had a small estate and no life insurance, so after all her debts were cleared, Gabe was left with about eight-hundred dollars. He joked that after he paid for a hotel room for the night, half of the money would be gone.

"Don't be ridiculous, Gabriel. You're not staying in any hotel when I have a super comfy couch," I told him, joking about how small my city apartment was. He reluctantly agreed after I insisted that he would never be an inconvenience to me, even after he stubbornly didn't speak to me for more than a month when I left Riverdale.

Gabe left after lunch on Saturday. With all the fancy restaurants in the city, you'd have thought he'd want to go out, but he requested his favorite cold weather meal and I made him just that—toasted cheese and tomato soup with tiny oyster crackers.

"Goodbye, Julia. It's been so nice to see you," he said. "Are you sure you don't want to come home with me?"

"Yes, I'm sure," I laughed. "I'll miss you, but I'm

planning to come home for Christmas, so maybe I'll see you then," I said as he was walking down the steps.

"Maybe?" he spun around. "You better see me then. Besides, I already have a present for you."

Just then his cab pulled up and I extended my arms to hug him. He held onto me, pressing my cheek against his chest and then he looked down at me and passionately kissed me on the lips. I was so stunned that I couldn't even bring myself to pull away. I stepped back and looked at him stupefied. He didn't say another word. Just got into the cab and drove away like nothing unordinary had happened.

I stood there for a moment, frozen. *What in the world did he do that for?* I asked myself. *Did I do something to mislead him?* No, there was no way I mislead him. I was sure of it. I would just have to ignore it and pretend it never happened. *But damn, that was a good kiss.*

Tom came over Monday after work. "So how was dinner with your old friend?" he asked sounding interested. But when I told him that Gabe stayed, he was furious.

"Why the hell didn't he get a room?"

"Because I have one here," I answered.

"I suppose you slept with him," he accused.

"I most certainly did not. It's not like that, Tom." I was defending the innocent nature of my relationship with Gabe but couldn't help thinking about his good-bye kiss.

"Oh I bet it isn't, you slut."

"Tom, for God's sake," I tried to explain that Gabe and I had been friends since childhood and that there had never been anything physical between us. Until that kiss, that is, but I of course didn't mention that.

"Well from now on, you and that Gabriel Jones won't be seeing anymore of each other when I'm not around." His eyes were piercing into mine and his authoritative tone was scaring me.

"Do you hear me?" he yelled, shaking my shoulders. I was baffled by his ugly display of possessiveness. This was a side of him I had not yet seen and one in which I never wanted to see again.

"I think you better leave," I said and waited until he did before the tears rolled down my cheeks.

When I got to the office the next day, a dozen long-stemmed red roses were on my desk. I was so furious with Tom from the night before that I just rolled my eyes and didn't even bother looking at the card. Flowers from Tom were the last thing I needed.

Halfway through the day, Anna made her way over and commented on the roses and how she wished she got flowers at work, just once, and how she wished she had a guy as incredible as Tom.

"No you don't, Anna," I said while typing away at my computer.

"Why? What happened?" she asked, and I told her about Tom's jealous outrage.

"That wasn't a very nice hello after he was gone all weekend. But at least he tried to make up for it."

Out of habit, she picked up the tiny envelope and opened the card. I didn't even look up from typing, but I knew Anna and I knew what she was doing.

"Julia," she said seriously. "These aren't from Tom."

"What?" I snapped. I stopped typing and grabbed for the card.

"Oh my word," was all I said but my mouth remained gaped. They were from Gabe. And the message said:

> "To my dearest Julia,
>> You don't always know what you have 'til it's gone. I miss you. With all my love and plenty more kisses to come.
>>> Love, Gabriel"

"Julia, was Tom right about you and Gabe?" Anna inquired.

"No, of course not. I don't know what Gabe's thinking. We're friends—that's all."

"I don't think he knows that," she said perceptively.

"I haven't seen him in two months. He dropped me off at the airport without saying goodbye, then he shows up and gives me the best kiss I've ever had and now this. I swear I have never led him on. He has always known that I felt our friendship was too important to ruin." I was rambling on like Anna, trying to make sense of Gabe's sudden advances toward me and figuring out what I might have done to provoke him.

"You probably didn't do anything then," she reassured me. "You probably acted just like yourself—

plain old Julia, and who knows what he would see in her," she said sarcastically.

I laughed. Anna had a great ability to always make my life seem not as bad as I saw it. Deep down I had known for quite some time that Gabriel loved me, but why the sudden indiscretion? And why the hell didn't Tom send flowers? He owed me an apology, dammit. Men. And everyone wondered why I had always despised dating.

Tom finally called a couple nights later to tell me he'd be going out of town for two weeks.

"So you won't be here for Thanksgiving?" I asked incredulously.

"No, I won't. I got a part in a play in Boston. I have to go. You understand, don't you?"

"Of course," I lied. I hadn't planned anything special, but I did expect to spend the holiday together. Now I'd be spending it alone. Oh well. I tried to convince myself that it didn't matter. I didn't like turkey anyway, but still I was disappointed.

"Maybe I could fly up for opening night," I suggested.

"That's okay, you're busy. I'll be back before you know it."

"When are you leaving?"

"Tomorrow. I'll call when I get there," he said flatly.

"Have a safe trip," I said and hung up the phone.

So there you have it. Earlier in the week I had been perplexed over the men in my life and now neither of them were anywhere in sight. Freedom or lone-liness? I was suddenly lonely. I decided to surprise Tom and fly to Boston the day before Thanksgiving so I could see his play and have dinner with him. There had been a winter weather advisory, but so far the snow hadn't yet begun. On the way to the airport, it was almost as if a thousand little powdered donuts suddenly burst from the sky. The snowflakes were giant and they were covering everything in sight, fall-ing quickly and effortlessly. The cab driver couldn't see the car in front of him and slammed on the brakes, causing the car to fishtail. The drive to LaGuardia took three times as long as normal, but I got there just in time to catch my flight. That is, if my flight hadn't been delayed, but it was. I waited three hours to board my plane, waiting for the snow to let up, but it didn't. Finally they canceled all flights and I waited another couple hours to get home. So I guess I'd be spending Thanksgiving alone after all.

It wasn't so bad. It gave me a lot of time to think. As much as I didn't want to admit it, I had fallen in love with Tom. At least I thought I was in love with him. For as much as I knew about being in love, any-way. I thought about him constantly and when he wasn't with me, I longed for his touch. I couldn't wait for our next encounter. And then there was the obvi-ous—charming, adorable and just plain good in bed.

Before I knew it, Christmas was almost near. I loved the holiday hustle and the way the snow glis-tened in the city lights. The mammoth tree in Rocke-feller Center was striking. Ever since I was a little girl, I had always wanted to go ice skating there, but Tom didn't like the cold and said it was too crowded. I was disappointed, but I didn't ask him again. Love is about compromise, I told myself.

I'd been shopping almost every night after work, trying to find the perfect gift for him. I never had any trouble buying presents for Gabe, but the truth was that even though I was in love with Tom and we shared the most intimate of moments, I really didn't know him all that well.

He had been so busy with his latest play showing four nights a week that I had hardly even seen him since before Thanksgiving. I went to opening night of each new show, but Tom preferred that I sit in the audience just like everyone else and leave right afterward. He didn't want any extra attention, he said. And he knew I had to get up early for work, so it was just as well. Besides, there were cast parties every night and he usually didn't get back until after dawn.

I wondered why his sister never came to see him perform since they seemed so close, but he said she had a baby and didn't really like the city. I had yet to meet her and his niece, but he kept saying that I would soon. His parents were a different story. He said they lived in the same town in Arizona, though they were divorced, and he hadn't seen either of them in years, so meeting them was out of the question.

With time dwindling away, I finally decided to buy him a nice watch and a polo shirt with the NBC logo on it since he mentioned on our first unofficial date that he hoped to someday star in one of their soaps. He was very talented. I knew he'd make it someday. Anna thought it was rude that he never invited me to any of the parties afterward, but I told her they were just for the cast. She disagreed, saying that she used to go to cast parties religiously with one of her ex-boyfriends. Sometimes Anna thought she knew everything.

CHAPTER FOUR

Two days before Christmas I flew home. Tom was supposed to come with me, but his sister got the flu and she needed him to help her take care of the baby. I was crushed. I offered to come with him, but he declined, saying that I should see my family and that we would have our own Christmas in New York when I got back.

My dad was waiting at the airport for me and his face lit up when he spotted me. I had missed him terribly, but I'd been too busy at work to dwell on it. Since I'd been gone, he retired from the post office and was once again volunteering at the fire department.

Traditionally, Gabe and I would spend Christmas Eve together ice skating in a town about thirty miles north of Riverdale and then he'd join me, dad and Grandpa Joe for dinner on Christmas Day. This year, I expected to be spending the day with Tom so I hadn't even bothered contacting Gabe—especially after Tom's jealous outrage after Gabe's visit in November. And then there was the kiss. I had just let it go, ignoring it, hoping it would go away. He must've done the same, probably even regretted it. But as much as I tried to discount his almighty kiss, I did think about it and wonder why. I pondered what to do, but there was only one thing I could think of. I was home and home meant Gabe. So I dialed his number and anxiously bit my bottom lip in anticipation of hearing his voice.

"Hi JC, it's been awhile," he said casually. *Casual, that's good.* After a long pause, he said exactly what I wanted to hear.

"So are you up for some skating?" he asked.

"You bet. Pick me up at seven and don't forget your gloves!"

Gabe had a habit of forgetting his gloves and would try to put his hands in my pockets to stay warm and we would end up toppling over on the ice and getting so cold that only hot chocolate could warm us up.

"If I do, I'll buy the cocoa," he laughed.

On the ride to the rink, we made idle chit-chat and neither of us mentioned Gabe's last goodbye to me or the flowers. Part of me felt like I should thank him for them and the other part wanted to ask him what the hell he was thinking and why he would do such a thing. My mind was at war with what to say, so I avoided it altogether.

While on the ice, my skate caught on a chunk of marred-up ice and I nearly fell, but Gabe caught me and helped me keep my balance. He was inches from my face and about to kiss me, I feared, when I blurted, "I've been seeing somebody!"

As soon as I said it, I regretted it. He looked so hurt. He stared at me for a minute then looked away before he said anything.

"What's his name?"

"Tom." There was no sense in hiding my relationship. I know it was silly, I guess it just seemed like a betrayal to Gabe.

"How long?" he asked, but I could tell he didn't really want to know the details.

"Since September." It really had been almost four months already.

"Why didn't you tell me about him when I was in New York?" He sounded agitated, like one feels when they're the last to know something.

"It never came up," I lied.

"Is it serious?"

"I think so," I said honestly. "I'm in love with him."

"That's great," Gabe said, but I know he didn't mean it. I could hear it in his voice.

"Ready for hot chocolate?" he asked.

"Gabe, I wanted to tell you. I just didn't know how."

"What's the big deal, Julia? You're a grown woman. You don't owe me any explanations for what you do with your life."

"No, I guess I don't. I mean, it's not like we're together that way," I stammered.

"Right. Just friends—isn't that what you always tell everybody?" He was clearly upset and I felt a sinking feeling inside. I never realized how insensitive it may have sounded to him when I'd set the record straight that we weren't a couple.

"So that's why you never cared about the flowers?" He asked after a minute of silence. Dang it, he went where I didn't want to go.

"It's not that I didn't care about them or about you," I explained. "It just surprised me and I didn't know what to think." He just stared at me, expressionless. I wiped a tear from the corner of my eye.

"Hot chocolate time," he announced abruptly.

So we went for hot chocolate. Gabe acted standoffish the whole time and when he dropped me off at my dad's house, I got out of the car without saying goodbye. I felt incredibly horrible. What bad timing I have. I should've known how much it would affect Gabe. What a lousy time to tell him. If only I had broken the news to him a month ago.

Grandpa Joe got up real early Christmas morning to cook. Ever since Grandma Ruth died, he had taken up preparing the holiday meals. The kitchen smelled great and the house looked festive. My dad had even hung up my stocking and filled it with gifts and I smiled when I found the orange at the bottom. He had done that every year and it warmed my heart that he kept up our simple tradition. It was good to be home. I enjoyed the afternoon with two of the most precious, stable men in my life. My heart was heavy though. Gabe never came over. Grandpa Joe didn't even need to ask why.

"Gabriel's upset over that boy you're seeing, isn't he?" he asked intuitively.

"Yes, Grandpa, but Tom's not a boy—he's twenty eight. And I'm not just seeing him, I'm in love with him."

"Oh child, don't put all your eggs in one basket." Grandpa Joe's clichés sometimes got on my nerves, but I could never be too annoyed with him.

"Don't worry about me, gramps. I'm a big girl."

Well, whoever said big girls don't cry? I cried myself to sleep that night upset over Gabriel's reaction to me being in love, but even more upset that Tom never even called to wish me a "Merry Christmas." I called his cell phone, but it just kept going to voicemail.

When I got back to the city, I called Anna to see how her holiday had been. There was a message on my machine from Tom apologizing for not calling, but that he'd been too wrapped up caring for his sister and all. Whatever. I was mad, but I was still looking forward to seeing him that night so I tried to forget about it. I knew, deep inside, that he didn't treat me that well. *You deserve better,* my inner voice told me. Yet, he had this strange hold on me. And when he walked into my apartment, all of my anger melted away.

"Hey babe," he said. "Miss me?"

"A little," I teased.

He kissed me and I leaned into him. I kissed him back, harder. We were hungry for each other.

Before we said another word, he was pushing himself against me and I could feel him growing bigger. I was getting more turned on by the second. He pushed me against the kitchen counter and lifted my sweater over my head. My nipples were already protruding in anticipation of his touch. He pulled my breast out of my bra and put his mouth on it, sucking it. He pinched my other nipple. He was rough, but I was getting wetter and wetter. I slithered out of my skirt and he lifted me onto the counter and stood in front of me. Without warning, he sank into me, pulled back and thrust again. It took my breath away. Deep. Hard. Over and over until my body convulsed — exploding with a tremendously strong orgasm. It was a sensation that transcended reality.

After returning to planet Earth, we sipped on eggnog while we exchanged our gifts.

"You first," he said and handed me a rectangular box.

I opened it quickly and gasped when I saw it. It was a beautiful silver and diamond bracelet with a dangling heart.

"It's gorgeous," I said examining it more closely. Then I saw the inscription on the back of the heart. It said: *"Yours, Preston."* Preston? Who was Preston? I handed it to Tom.

"Whose Preston?" I asked, puzzled.

He hesitated for a moment and shifted his eyes

from the bracelet to me. "I meant to tell you," he said.

"Tell me what?"

"I'm changing my name," he answered nonchalantly.

"You're *what*?"

"I wanted a stage name with more pizzazz, more attitude," he said.

I took a moment to absorb his explanation and contemplate this sudden name change before I gave him his gift. Preston. It did sound more Hollywood. But he should've inscribed it with *Tom*. To me, he was Tom. I was in love with Tom, not Preston. I was still dwelling on this long after he left. *Something is not right here,* my inner voice was provoking me, making me doubt my trusting instinct. *So the gift may have not been perfect,* I told her, *but the sex sure was.*

Anna noticed my bracelet right away.

"Good heavens Jules, are you trying to blind me?" she giggled.

The diamonds caught the sunlight and cast off prisms around my desk.

"Can I try it on?" she asked, totally serious.

Laughing, I undid the clasp and handed it over. She read the inscription and gave me a cock-eyed look.

"Who the hell is Preston?"

"Tom," I said, but she ignored me.

"This says 'Yours, Preston.' How many boyfriends do you have? You can send a couple my way, you know. And here I was hoping that you had a nice

Christmas. You sure spread yourself thin. Tom is gonna flip out if he sees this."

I let her go on and on until she finally stopped for air.

"So who's Preston?" she asked, furrowing her brow.

"Preston is Tom," I said again.

"He's *who*?"

"Tom. He thought it made a better stage name or something like that," I explained.

"Oh, I see," she said incredulously and handed the bracelet back to me, stepping backwards until she ran into my filing cabinet.

I just shook my head. "Anna, really. Tom gave me the bracelet last night. Trust me, I'd tell you if Preston was some knight in shining armor who gave diamonds to women he didn't even know."

"You'd better!" she yelled as she walked away.

Anna sure was a trip. Always jumping to conclusions. Always skeptical. That was Anna.

CHAPTER FIVE

In early March, Tom—er I mean Preston—had a series of auditions. He didn't tell me until afterward that he had even tried out for a part in a new soap opera. He had long since quit waiting tables at Casablanca and was diving headfirst into as many performances as he could.

Gabe and I hadn't spoken since the night we went ice-skating before Christmas. The gift I bought him was still wrapped and lying in the bottom drawer of my dresser. I thought several times about calling him, but I wouldn't know what to say. I didn't think I owed him any apologies. After all, who was he to judge me?

LAURA LEIGH LESKOVAC

Why couldn't he be happy for me? Still, I felt bad with the way everything had turned out.

I was at work writing an article on the declining number of car thefts in the city when Tom—dammit, Preston—called with his good news. He had been asked back for a second audition for *St. Louis Blues*, the newest soap to debut on daytime television. He got the part. I was so happy for him that I jumped out of my chair and unconsciously drew everyone's attention to myself. We went out to a club that night and celebrated hard. So hard that I didn't make it into work the next morning.

The first vodka shots went down so easily, and before I knew it, I was drunk and ready for a wild time. I motioned for Tom to follow me to the dance floor. I was lost in the music and I let the rhythm take over my body. I was moving in sync to the techno sounds and rubbing my backside against him, his front to my back. I could feel his hardness. I turned to face him and ran my hand down his chest and clutched his crotch, right there amidst the crowded floor. It was so erotic. Sweat was forming on my forehead and on my neck. I was hot. So hot and bothered. He whispered in my ear: "I want you. Now." The urgency in his voice turned me on even more. I kissed him lustfully, slipping my tongue into his mouth. I was ready for him. I wanted him. I needed him.

"Let's go," I said and grabbed his hand, leading him out of the side door of the club. We no sooner exited when he pulled me into him and kissed me so hard that my lips felt numb. We stumbled into the alley and found privacy under some construction scaffolding that was enclosed with thick opaque plastic. I leaned over a cold, metal bar and held onto it to steady myself. I was dizzy, either from the alcohol or the sexual tension. Tom stood behind me, put his hands on my waist, reached under my skirt and pulled my panties to the side. *Ahhhh, yes please, this is just what I wanted.* I panted as he slid one finger, then two inside of me.

"Spread your legs," he commanded and I all too willingly obliged.

With my panties still pulled to the side and him behind me, he plummeted inside and pumped in and out until I let out a loud squeal of pleasure and delight. It was reckless and uninhibited. And oh so good.

St. Louis Blues was going to tape soon. Preston was going to play a tennis coach at the elite country club who would eventually capture the heart of one of the leading ladies. It suited him well. Anna asked me if I'd be jealous watching his on-screen trysts with other women. I said I wouldn't. I had already encountered much of that with his plays over the past six months. A stage kiss is nothing like the real thing, I told her. I admit—it was hard at first. It would be a lie if I said I never felt a pang of jealousy, but I could deal with it. All I had to do was remind myself that although it appeared Preston was having a steamy romance with some beautiful actress, it was actually me he was with. It was my body he touched so sensually—it was me he took to dizzying heights of gratification.

The first tapings were for the soap's pilot and Preston was gone sixteen hours a day. After an intensive three weeks, he got a break and we retreated to Connecticut for the weekend. This time we stayed at a four-star hotel and our room had a hot tub. The first night was unforgettable. Preston said he needed to unwind and that some steam would do wonders for his tense muscles. Boy did it ever. We went to the lower level of the hotel where the sauna was and went in together. I kneaded his aching shoulders and massaged every single inch of his body. We were dripping with sweat. We were so hot for each other that we fucked right there. We went from the sauna to the deserted swimming pool and fucked again. He sat on the steps in the shallow end and pulled himself out of his swim trunks, tempting me. I was insatiable, so I pulled my bikini bottom aside and straddled him, impaling myself on his raging hard-on. *God did it feel good!* The buoyancy of the water made it so easy for me to naturally bob up and down on him. *Oh, what a slippery, incredible sensation.*

Neither of us cared if anyone saw us. We were too self-absorbed in our indulgence in each other. I never thought of myself as an exhibitionist, as Anna once pointed out to me after I divulged to her the juicy details of our public fornication the night we partied hard. It was just that I had an uncontrollable desire for him. It was a carnal need that surpassed any logical explanation.

The night commenced after hours of pleasuring each other and the next night ended in much the same way. We got back to the city late Sunday night and I went to bed feeling relaxed and in love. The next day I was enraged and distressed.

There was a copy of a soap opera tabloid on my desk opened to an article on *St. Louis Blues*. It was complete with an overview of the show's storyline and biographies of each of the new stars. My jaw nearly hit the floor when I saw Preston's picture and accompanying information.

"Playing the part of Marcus VanHorn is Preston Thomason Ford, 28. Ford resides in New Jersey with his wife Marissa. The couple has a two-year-old daughter Jessica and another baby on the way. In his spare time, Ford enjoys weightlifting and skiing. He has performed in nearly 70 plays before making his debut on St. Louis Blues."

I was numb. I was frozen. To say I was upset would be a gross understatement. I just sat there, staring at his photograph in disbelief. *Yes, this looked like my Tom, but who was this guy?* There had to be some mistake. His sister lived in New Jersey with her daughter. The article meant to say his *sister*, not his *wife*. I was in denial. *I told you so,* my inner voice gloated. And he enjoyed skiing? He hated the cold, he told me. My mind flashed back to when I asked him to go ice skating. This must be a mistake, too. Careless reporters misquoted people all the time. *Calm down, Julia,* I told myself. *There's a rational explanation for all of this.* Still, I couldn't help feeling like my world had just turned upside-down.

Anna came bouncing over talking a mile a minute about her date over the weekend before she sat down and saw that something was wrong.

'"Julia, are you okay? You don't look well."

I couldn't answer her. I was there, but I wasn't.

"Julia! What happened? What's the matter?" she asked and yanked the magazine from my death grip, ripping the corner of the page.

"Oh my God!" she gasped. "What are you going to do?"

"About what?" I asked, unfazed by her agonizing tone of voice.

"About what?" she shrieked. "Julia, are you coherent?"

I stared blankly at Anna as she sat across from me.

"I thought you said he was always going to see his sister in Jersey. Didn't you ever meet her?" she asked.

"Nope. Never got around to it."

"We're reporters, Julia. We can handle this. We'll get to the bottom of it. What's her name?"

Anna was flighty most of the time, but she had her head on her shoulders when it counted and I was grateful she was able to be my rock.

"Her name is Hannah, he said. I don't know her last name. She has a baby, I guess, but I don't know if she was married..." my voice broke off. I guess I didn't really know anything. I had been thinking with my heart and not my head. *You mean you were thinking with your libido!* Damn voice in my head. But I was afraid she was right.

"I'm sorry, Julia. We'll figure this out." Anna got to work right away, not on her *Times* story, but on our own investigation. She checked around and couldn't find any listings for a Hannah Ford, but that didn't mean much because we weren't sure if she and Preston shared the same last name. Hell, who knew if there was even a sister at all! Anna did find a listing for a Marissa Ford who was named in the article as his wife. We had a number but weren't sure what to do with it.

"Should I call her or do you want to?" Anna asked me, her eyes darting around, trying to avoid contact with mine. We had too much work to do with deadlines looming so we couldn't take off and drive there, which I would've preferred to do, but there was no way I would jeopardize my job over this.

"I'll call her," I said boldly. It was my problem— my huge problem.

The phone rang several times before a woman picked up. I could hear a baby crying in the background.

"Hello?" she answered. I was silent. "Hello?"

I could sense she was about to hang up, so I spoke.

"Hi," I said slowly. "May I please speak to Marissa Ford?"

"This is she. Who's calling?"

"My name is uh Anna," I improvised. "I'm calling from the *New York Times* and I'd just like to ask you a couple of questions if that's okay." I pretended to be doing a story on the new soap opera.

"Ask away," she said politely and gave me the green light.

"About your relationship with Preston Ford," I

began cautiously.

"Yes? What about it?"

"How, how long have the two of you been married?" *Please say you're not married. Please laugh and say I've got it all wrong. I can't be sleeping with a married man. Please validate my instincts. I couldn't have been this wrong about somebody. Please tell me this is all a cruel joke.* That didn't happen.

"We've been married for three years," she said. That was all I heard and I dropped the phone. That was all I needed to hear.

"What'd she say, Julia? What is it?" Anna was genuinely concerned.

"It was his wife," I choked on my own tears.

"That son of a bitch," she said through clenched teeth.

"How could he do this? Who the hell did he think he was fooling?" she asked.

"Me, Anna. That's who." I couldn't believe it myself, but I had to.

Tom, Preston, whoever the hell he was, came to my apartment later that evening, unaware that I had seen the magazine article. I let him in, but pulled back when he tried to kiss me. I loathed him at that moment. Who did he think he was—a married man waltzing into my life and sweeping me off of my feet.

"Julia, what's up? Something wrong?" he asked without a clue that I finally knew about his dual life.

"Why don't you tell me?" I asked snidely.

"Don't play games. Just tell me what's bothering

you."

Me play games? Ha! If only. It was almost laughable, although it wasn't at all funny. I threw the magazine at him and walked into the kitchen to pour myself another glass of wine. I had been drinking since I got home, which I didn't ordinarily do, but I was hurt and miserable and this was anything but ordinary—so why not? How anybody could put another through this kind of heartache and pain was beyond me. It was cruel and selfish.

As soon as he opened his mouth to explain, I held up my hand. I knew there would only be more lies gushing out. That's all the past eight months had been—lies.

"I don't even want to hear it," I said. "Everything about you is a lie—even your name. Preston. A stage name, ha! You make me sick, you son of a bitch. And the bracelet you gave me... guess you royally screwed up there, didn't you? Of course you did!" I was answering my own questions as fast as I shot them out.

"It was meant to be hers, wasn't it? Wasn't it?!?" I shouted. I was crying uncontrollably by this point. I had taken off the bracelet the instant I walked in the door and put it on the counter. I picked it up and flung it at him.

"Get out!" I yelled.

"I never meant to hurt you, Julia," he said. And without further repentance, he was gone.

When life seems too good to be true, it usually is. Just as Anna had suspected all along, Tom was a rat. I was so mad at myself for letting my guard down, for letting him in, for falling so hard. And I felt so dirty, so used. Damn him. Damn him for tearing down my fortress. Damn him for breaking my heart.

I was listening to Billy Joel and feeling sorry for myself, but when I listened to the words of *And So It Goes*, I quit crying and instead, got angrier by the second. *"In every heart, there is a room; a sanctuary safe and strong, to heal the wounds of lovers past, until a new one comes along..."* How ridiculous is that? It sounded so foolish. What kind of woman falls prey to one man and recovers just long enough to fall prey to another? A weak one, that's who. Not me. Not ever again. My grandpa used to say that falling in love and the pain of the aftermath was like falling off a horse. It hurts a lot and it may take some time to heal, but you can't let your fear of falling stop you from ever riding again, he said. I, however, wondered if riding was worth the pain. As far as I was concerned, these stable doors were closed.

CHAPTER SIX

Most people have someone they run to when nothing else in life seems worth living for. For me that someone was Gabe. I had planned to go home to Riverdale for Easter. I took a couple personal days so I could extend my stay to five days, giving me some time to recuperate from the agony and pain of Tom's betrayal.

I arrived on Good Friday and went straight to my father's house. Gabe and I hadn't spoken since December, but once he heard what happened with Tom, he'd probably forget all about our little spat and welcome me home with open arms. I brought along the Christmas present I had never given him, figuring it could be a peace offering.

The day before Easter was sunny, yet breezy and cool. I put on a light jacket and set out to get Grandpa Joe and dad their traditional chocolate bunnies from their favorite chocolate shop. Neither of them used to have much of a sweet tooth, but Grandpa said the older he got, the more he liked to nibble on something sweet before he went to bed. Dad had almost become the same way. I also got Gabe a chocolate egg filled with coconut. It had always been his favorite.

I drove over to Gabe's house to surprise him. There was an unfamiliar car in his driveway, so I parked across the street and just as I was about to open my door, Gabe and a woman I didn't recognize walked out of the garage and stopped beside her car. They hugged and Gabe held her chin in his hand and kissed her passionately while I sank down into my seat, trying to remain unnoticed.

An unexpected pang of jealousy hit me as I stared at them. She looked very pretty in her strappy Spring dress and sandals. She had short, blonde hair and drove a red convertible—not Gabe's usual type. I wondered if she was as smart as the outfit she wore on this fifty-degree day.

As soon as she left, I waited until Gabe went back inside before I drove away. He had moved on and it wouldn't have been fair for me to just barge into his life whenever it was convenient for me. I waited until after dinner on Sunday to drop off the chocolate I got for him. He wasn't home, which was a relief, so I left the chocolate in his garage beside the door that led inside. He'd be sure to see it there. I didn't want to keep another gift for him in my dresser. Then I went back to New York.

The city sure seemed a world away from Riverdale. I came back to the insane traffic, the non-stop honking and the usual daily chaos. Home sweet home. I didn't like the city anymore. I guess because everything I thought it would be, wasn't.

I had imagined marrying Tom and meeting him occasionally at Rick's Café for lunch, where we first met. We'd have crazy, uninhibited sex in all kinds of places. Our sex life wouldn't fizzle like in Anna's marriage. We would love having sex together as often as possible. I fantasized about us riding naked on our horses along the beach and rolling around in the sand, making love.

What a joke. I suppose I dream too much, or perhaps I dream idealistically and not realistically, but isn't that what imaginations are for? I was once told that anticipation is always greater than the realization. The idea scared me so much that I've remembered it after all these years and have reflected upon it on many occasions.

Here I was, alone. Again. No more nightly phone calls, no more plays, no more weekends in Connecticut. The days wore on endlessly. Work was all I had in this city where I didn't belong. How I longed for Grandpa Joe's infamous chili, for evening walks with my dad, for horseback rides with Gabe.

I was desperate for companionship. I argued with myself about my feelings for Tom. Was it really love anyway? *He never said he loved you, Julia. You only said it after sex. He was nothing more than a bad habit. An ad-*

diction. You didn't make love—you fucked. My inner self had a voice of reason. *Sometimes.* She was right, though. He never did say he loved me. And did we ever make love? I hadn't thought so much about it when we were together. Did I mistake lust for love?

I had too much time to think and to dwell on the big, foolish mistake I made. Anna said she had enough of my self-deprecation and insisted on setting me up with someone. I went on numerous blind dates, at her insistence, until I threatened to never talk to her again if she didn't stop. They were all either reformed drug addicts, unemployed or still married. One talked about his therapist so much that I wondered if he was in love with her. Where were all the "normal" men? I wasn't drop-dead gorgeous, but I wasn't chopped liver either. I was slender with a curvaceous body. I had joined a gym shortly after moving to NYC and since my breakup with Tom, I had let my hair grow long again. I had a pretty face, a keen fashion sense and a successful career. So where did I go wrong?

Anna had found the perfect guy for her. He was tall and lean—too thin for my tastes—but they complemented each other well. He had a good job as a buyer for a top-notch clothing store, which was much more ambitious than her ex. She was really happy. I'd never seen her so giddy.

They included me often on their outings, but I had begun to feel like a third wheel and they needed some time to get to know each other better without me hovering, so I started going everywhere solo. I had been wanting to see a Broadway play, but I just couldn't bring myself to going alone. I had finally broken down and gotten a ticket to see *Cats*—can you believe I had never seen it—but I never made it there. A devastating phone call minutes before my cab was due to arrive sent me crashing to the floor. I fainted as soon as I heard, "...terrible accident. It's your grandpa... and your father."

When I came to, I called Anna who rushed me to the airport and insisted on coming with me. We hopped on the first plane to Ohio. Gabe had been the one who called. I was still in shock when Anna and I raced into the emergency-room entrance of the only hospital in Riverdale. I asked the not-so-friendly woman at the registration desk where I could find John and Joe Baker. She told me to have a seat and that a doctor would talk to me shortly. Have a seat? Are you kidding me? I had so many unanswered questions swirling around in my mind.

The waiting room was full of police officers and men I recognized from the fire station. They looked tired and solemn. One of them gave me an understanding nod and I nodded in reply. Gabe was sitting in a chair with his arm draped over the shoulder of the blonde-haired woman I had seen him with months before. He made a beeline across the room as soon as he saw me and hugged me tight. I rested my head against his chest. It was then that I fell apart. I had been patient and strong before that. I had kept it together. Now the tears came and I could do nothing to stop them.

"What happened?" I asked between sobs.

"There was a fire," Gabe said softly and slowly as if he were talking to a child. "Your dad wasn't home."

"Then where is he?" I interrupted. "He's okay, then?"

"JC, listen to me," he said sternly. "Your dad ran into the house to get your grandfather and there was an explosion."

"Oh God, are they, did they…" I couldn't finish my sentence. I glanced at one of the firemen who was wiping his face with a tissue. Had he been crying, too? Why? What didn't I know?

"Gabe?" I asked, pleading with my eyes for him to tell me what he clearly didn't want to say.

"Grandpa Joe didn't make it, Julia."

"What about my dad?" I asked with my heart beating so rapidly I thought it would race right out of my chest.

"He's alive, but I got to tell you that it's not good, JC. They don't know if he's going to pull through," Gabe said firmly. He was always so strong—always my rock. I don't know what I would've done if he hadn't been there. I forgot all about Anna and Gabe's girlfriend. It was just the two of us against the world, like it always had been. It was just the two of us there in that waiting room, at least that's how it seemed. Tragedy has a strange way of bringing people back together despite the time lost from what seemed so trivial in comparison. At that moment, I couldn't remember why Gabe and I had become strangers over the past year. None of that mattered now. All that mattered was that Gabe was here with me when I needed him the most.

Anna fell asleep reading a newspaper and I had just gotten back from the bathroom when the doctor came in and told me that my father was in the intensive care unit.

"I want to prepare you for what you're about to see," the doctor began. "Your father has third-degree burns on the right side of his body, including his face. He has a feeding tube and a lot of machines helping him survive. The risk of infection is very high, so you must be entirely sterilized before entering his room. Do you understand?"

"Yes," I said, shaking my head.

"When we feel he is more stable, he will be transferred to a burn trauma center. Until then, we have made him as comfortable as possible. You can see him now, but he will most likely go in and out of consciousness. He's on a lot of pain medications. He may be able to hear you though." The doctor spoke to me gently and muttered his condolences for my grandfather.

That night was the longest night of my life. A couple nurses helped me dress to see my father. Even though the doctor had warned me about what to expect, no one can prepare you to see your father, your hero, so helpless and fragile. How ironic it was that my father had devoted most of his life to fighting fires and in the end, fire destroyed his own house, killed my grandpa and caused my dad to be fighting for his life. Of course it wasn't just the fire that put him there. It was also bravery and love. I had gathered from the staff and local newspaper reporters that my father had been at the fire station for a summer party when the call came through, dispatching crews to 42 Maple Drive—my childhood address. The other firefighters urged my dad to stay, but he couldn't be stopped. When they arrived at the house, the upper level was already engulfed in flames. My dad charged in without hesitation. Three other men ran in as well, but they smelled gas and one of them ran out to evacuate the neighborhood. The other two started up the stairs for my dad and grandpa when they heard an explosion. It was too early to determine the cause of the fire, the fire marshal said, but it was suspected to be natural gas. A freak accident, I was told. A freak accident that took away my dear old grandpa.

It was hard to believe that I'd never see him again. Easter had been the last time I saw him. He was happily devouring his chocolate bunny when we sat down to have one of our heart-to-heart talks. Grandpa Joe was the most perceptive and practical person I knew and he loved me deeply. He was my confidant and I had told him all about Tom. He was furious. He said that Tom wouldn't know a gem if it knocked him square in the jaw. He was biased, of course, but I didn't mind. We talked for a long time that night, but I would have kept him up even later had I known it would be the last time I'd seek refuge in his wisdom and sensibility.

"Don't look at life through rose-colored glasses, Julia. See people for who they are," he said—his last words of advice. I cried softly, thinking of him and Grandma Ruth and my poor father who was so vulnerable right now. Gabe took me back to his house and extended an invitation to stay as long as I needed to, but I wanted to be alone, so I stayed only long enough to splash some cold water in my face, drink a cup of tea and call Riverdale's only inn.

Three days later, my father died. My sorrow was immeasurable. He passed away in transit to the burn center. The doctor said he was just too weak to survive. I thought I was, too. Anna and Gabe helped make all the arrangements. We held the funerals together, just like dad and grandpa had been all those years. Grandpa Joe already had a burial spot reserved next to grandma's and I wanted my dad's as close to theirs as possible. They each had a handsome life insurance that more than covered expenses, so I had no worries monetarily. There was insurance on the house as well, but all that money was no consolation to losing two of the most precious people in my life. All of the riches in the world couldn't replace my loss.

After all the loose ends were tied up, I had nothing to do but go back to New York. The fire made me an orphan. All alone. No family. Just me. The only person I had in Riverdale was Gabe and he had Cara. I needed to work anyway. I couldn't mope around all day dwelling on how empty my life had suddenly become.

The Times had three reporters out on maternity leave, so there were extra assignments and I took them all. Everyone at work had been so kind and caring since the accident, especially Anna. She and her boyfriend forced me to get out of the house at least once a week, and as much as I tried to decline, I was glad for it. I had become a very private person—boring to be perfectly honest. Reading had become my salvation. My favorite authors got me through the sleepless nights I spent alone. I thought about getting a cat. I hadn't had one since childhood. I smiled, remembering my fat orange cat Whiskers. *Don't get a cat. Don't be a lonely cat lady*, my inner voice told me. And I listened to her, for it seemed like an easy trap to fall into.

The only calls I ever got were from Anna or Ross, neither of whom could truly understand the depth of my grief. Gabe called about once a month, but our conversations never lasted long. He would ask how I was doing, I'd lie and say I was fine. He would ask about work and I would ask about his students. He skirted around asking me about my social life and he was very evasive when it came to Cara. Our talks were unemotional, distant. I was intentionally aloof. Part of me was envious, I suppose, that he had someone. The other part of me resented him in a way for so selfishly risking our friendship for an impractical romance. I had always been so careful, so restrained when it came to thinking of him as more. I wanted him to be my friend without any awkwardness between us, and he ruined that. Now we had an uncomfortable, strained relationship and uneasy conversation. It was clear that I would never have the friend in him that I once had, that I once held so dear.

CHAPTER SEVEN

Almost a year went by before I was able to laugh again. And then it happened. It was June. The *Times* assigned me to cover a story on a city psychologist who had recently published a book on a body image disorder. His book was controversial because it challenged a renowned psychologist's decades-old research that this mental health condition was imaginary. Rather, the book was calling for the psychiatric community to recognize it as a disorder treatable by proper medication. Or something like that. Blah, blah, blah.

I was to attend a lecture by the psychologist on the topic at Cornell University in Ithaca on a Thursday evening and write an article on his findings.

B-O-R-I-N-G. It didn't interest me in the least. I tried all I could do to get re-assigned, but my efforts were in vain. I had three days to learn as much as I could on the psychologist and the supposed disorder. That was the part I both loved and hated about being a reporter. The preliminary information-gathering was necessary to write a good, thorough story and I enjoyed being knowledgeable in many areas, but the times restraints were always so limiting. I would have to spend the next two nights reading Dr. Nicholas Stanton's new book and researching all the background on him and the subject so I would know what questions to ask without sounding like a fool, like a schoolgirl who failed to do her homework. No, that wasn't me. Only stupid people ask stupid questions.

And that's just what I did.

I took a seat in the auditorium in the section reserved for media and fiddled with my pen and notebook. Yawning, I readjusted my blouse and sat up straighter. All around me were stuffy people in stuffy suits. What a bore. I was beginning to get cabin fever and needed to get out more, but this surely was no cure.

Then Dr. Stanton entered the room and all eyes shifted to him. He was incredibly good looking. Much more so than his picture. I was immediately drawn to him. I felt as if he could see right through me, as if he'd known me in a lifetime before.

After his presentation, reporters and members of the medical community fired questions at him.

"Dr. Stanton, is this more common in patients

who also have schizophrenia?", "Dr. Stanton, how many people do you surmise suffer from this disease?", "Dr. Stanton, are there any correlations between this disorder and OCD?"

And then it was my turn. With my hand raised eagerly, he looked straight at me.

"Dr. Stanton, are you free tomorrow night?"

That wasn't the question I had in mind — it just came out. My peers all looked at me as if I had committed the ultimate taboo. But what did I have to lose? I knew from reading his bio that he was single and lived in lower Manhattan. He was obviously smart and incredibly aristocratic. Why he wasn't married, I didn't know, but from what I had read, he had just looked for love in all the wrong places.

An eternity seemed to pass before he answered my question.

"No, Miss. Not anymore," he said grinning.

After the q & a session, he pushed right through the crowd of lingering reporters to get to me.

"Nicholas Stanton," he said as he extended his hand.

"Julia Baker. Nice to meet you, doctor."

"Likewise," he said and glanced around the room. "So what time shall I be ready tomorrow evening?"

The contrast between his crisp, white shirt and his navy blue suit jacket looked stunning on him. He had dark brown hair and deep-set brown eyes with a few tiny freckles across the bridge of his nose. He was nearly ten years my senior, but he looked ageless.

"How about seven?" I asked after a long pause. Dang, I think I was staring at him.

"Seven works," he said. "What did you think of my research?"

"Fascinating," I said truthfully. What began as boring medical findings instantly and unexpectedly became interesting. We exchanged numbers and we agreed to meet at his place in the financial district. Anna would be so proud.

I stayed up late that night writing my article. I wrote very meticulously all the time, but on this piece, I was extra cautious. I knew Dr. Stanton would be reading it scrupulously. It also took longer than usual because my eyes kept averting to my closet. What in the world was I going to wear? I couldn't think of a single thing I owned that would be perfect. I had been so depressed that I hadn't gone shopping in quite some time. Anna had tried on countless occasions to get me interested in the sale at Macy's or Saks', but I didn't bite. I had nowhere to go but to work and I had plenty of office clothes.

Since my father and grandfather had died, I had changed. It had gotten to the point where I almost didn't recognize myself. Then, suddenly, Nicholas Stanton steps into my life and my biggest worry was my aged wardrobe. I called Anna right away and she said we'd go on an emergency shopping trip during lunch the next day. I was appeased enough to finish the article and get some sleep. Anna always knew what to say.

Friday morning was a struggle to get up. I must've pressed the snooze button at least a half a dozen times before forcing myself to get out of bed. I looked in the mirror as I brushed my teeth. Oh, I looked tired. I definitely could've used some more beauty rest—that's for sure.

As promised, Anna went shopping with me and helped me ward off the ever-so-persistent salespeople. Oh yes, I did need help, but much more than they could offer me. I didn't even know where to begin. Did I want to look intelligent? Cute? Sexy?

"You have to dress for the occasion," Anna said. "It's just a date."

"This is much more than a date, Anna. Tonight I'm meeting the man I'm going to marry," I said boldly and laughed.

"My goodness, someone sounds sure of herself. Welcome back, Julia," she said and winked.

I *was* back. Even though I didn't get enough sleep, I had woken up refreshed and optimistic. I was suddenly rejuvenated and I *could* live happily again, couldn't I? For the first time since the fire, I didn't feel guilty for being excited about something.

I tried on skirts, shorts, pants, dresses and a dozen shirts before I found what I was looking for. I decided to go for the "I'm trendy and available look" by buying an above-the-knee black sleeveless dress. You could never go wrong with black. It was classic. Anna found me the sexiest pair of silver heels while I completed the ensemble with a new pair of silver teardrop earrings and matching necklace. I was absolutely tickled with my purchases and practically skipped back to the office.

Anna suggested that I make reservations at a restaurant that she and Dolen frequented, but it was already booked so I called Mozzarelli's Bistro and asked for a secluded booth. I wanted my date all to myself. I was dying to get to know him better. I knew I shouldn't set my hopes high. I knew I'd probably just be setting myself up for disappointment. There's that old "anticipation is always greater than the realization" thing I was talking about. He was more than likely going to turn out to be a creep just like all the others. I knew he wasn't gay, so what else could be wrong with him? The list in my mind was endless. Former porn star, escaped convict with a new identity, an alcoholic, a transsexual. I told myself to stop. *Not this one, Julia, not this one.* I wanted him to be every bit as wonderful as I had hoped. And for once, he proved to be.

Meeting him at his penthouse was a little awkward. I waited in the air-conditioned lobby while the doorman buzzed him. He didn't answer. I suddenly felt foolish standing there. Maybe he changed his mind and decided not to go after all. Maybe he just accepted last night to be polite. Maybe he didn't like the article I had written. Maybe he didn't find me attractive. Maybe I should just stop while I'm ahead.

"I don't think this darn thing's working," the doorman said. "I'll have to call him."

After a few seconds he apologized for the wait and said that Dr. Stanton was on his way down. Maybe I should breathe a sigh of relief.

When the elevator doors opened, out stepped the love of my life. I kid you not. At that exact moment, I fell head over heels. I know it sounds ridiculous. I just can't explain it. You know that lump in your throat when you're about to get kissed for the first time. Yep, it was there. Feelings that I never had before surged through me like electricity through a live wire. It was dangerous. I was ashamed of myself for falling so fast. I knew it was stupid and irrational, but I had no control over it. Maybe somebody else had taken over my body. Where was the sensible Julia I had known my whole life? You would've thought I learned after the whole Tom debacle. But no. I was just as vulnerable as ever and setting myself up for further regression, I feared. I had to contain myself so he wouldn't know how much he intrigued me, how attracted I was to him, how I planned to be his wife. That would no doubt scare him away. *Stop staring, Julia,* I told myself. *And for goodness sake, say something.*

"Hi," was all that came out. What an idiot.

"How are you?" he asked casually.

"I'm fine, thank you." Okay, so I was at a loss for words. There's a first time for everything.

"Is that our cab?" he asked, pointing toward the street.

"Yes, we have reservations at Mozzarelli's. Have you been there?"

"No, I don't think so. I love Italian, though. How'd you know?" He said jokingly. His smile was incredibly contagious. I couldn't help but grin. Chalk one up for me. Anna's place was Mediterranean.

"I read the article, by the way," he said. Uh-oh, I didn't think he'd bring it up so soon.

"And?" I asked curiously.

"I was very pleased with it," he said seriously. "You are the first reporter I've met that really seems to understand the importance of my research."

"I'm glad you liked it." I was so relieved.

Dinner went smoothly, except for one minor faux pas. I ordered the fettuccini alfredo and he chose the eggplant parmesan. After we finished our salads, our meals arrived and I tightly twirled my fettuccini around my fork so that I wouldn't lose any of it on the way from my plate to my mouth. I looked over at him and smiled before opening my mouth to eat my forkful and would you know, one damn noodle escaped from my utensil and slid down, leaving a trail of white sauce from my chin to my chest—right where it landed. I dipped the edge of my cloth napkin into my water to clean up my mess and accidentally overturned the glass, spilling it onto the table where it was mostly absorbed by the tablecloth, except for the little bit that went right over the edge and onto Nick's lap. I was mortified. I apologized profusely and quickly summoned a waiter, all the while trying to remain calm, trying to look elegant. As if. What a klutz. Nick laughed and delicately teased that grace was not an essential quality on his perfect-woman list. I eased a bit and joked to him that if it had been a prerequisite, I would have had to rescind my dinner invitation to him.

"You have the laugh of an angel," he said and instantly the embarrassment faded.

Despite that mishap, the food was delicious and the conversation couldn't have gone better. We talked as if we were old friends. I loosened up after a couple glasses of red wine. He seemed more than relaxed and even declined a third glass. Nope—he wasn't an alcoholic. I could cross that one off my list. When the waiter brought the check, he scooped it up without hesitation. What wasn't there to like about this guy? I, however, insisted on paying.

"I invited you to dinner," I reminded him.

"You just got around to it first, kid," he said. There was that smile again.

"Kid?" I flirted by smiling coyly, but I was taken aback by his reference. There was an age difference, but it wasn't outright obvious. I wondered if it made him uncomfortable. Well if so, he didn't let it bother him for long.

It was a gorgeous summer night so after dinner we walked to Central Park and Nick asked if I'd like to go on a carriage ride with him. Yes, a carriage ride. This date was straight out of a romance movie—the kind I cynically thought never existed, except for on the big screen. Two beautiful white horses led us through the streets of lower Manhattan. It was very romantic. He even bought me a red rose. Could you blame me for falling so fast? The night commenced when I stepped out of the taxi. He also got out, but just to kiss me good-night on the cheek.

"I'll call you," he said sincerely. Then he took the cab home. He didn't suggest a nightcap and neither did I. I didn't want things to move that quickly. I lay in bed for a while that Friday night, restless, replaying the evening in my mind until sleep got the best of me.

When I woke up the next morning, my apartment suddenly felt dull and dismal. I guess it had suited my mood for the past year. I had even hung dark blinds on the windows to keep the sun from entering. But on this day, I opened them. I opened the windows as wide as they could open and stood there, in the sun-light, feeling alive once again. The early summer tem-peratures had been mild all week and a subtle breeze was blowing the curtains. I walked around as if in someone else's home and discarded anything that no longer pleased me, including Tom's ashtray. I had got-ten rid of all his stuff long ago, but I hadn't been able to bring myself to let go of the bright red ashtray we bought in Chinatown. I didn't smoke and I hated it when he did. It was a filthy habit, but he looked damn sexy with a cigarette so I tolerated it. Funny the things we overlook when we're in love or in lust, whatever it was. Oh well. Today even the ashtray met its demise.

I was starting over—today. I put on a Simon & Garfunkel CD, my favorite, and sang along as I rear-ranged furniture and dusted all that had been neglect-ed for so long. I wondered when and if Nick would call. I figured he would wait, not wanting to sound too eager to see me again. To pass the time, I went shop-ping. I splurged on myself, buying new summer clothes, sunglasses and three pairs of flipflops. I de-cided the apartment could use some sprucing up, too, so I bought candles, fresh flowers, two plants, a lamp and a summery quilt with sunflowers on it.

I ate pepperoni pizza for lunch and a double-scoop chocolate almond ice cream cone afterward. I indulged in anything I wanted to. I was having fun. Fun. Did I say that? For the first time since my dad and Grandpa Joe died, I was enjoying life and all of its simple pleasures.

I wasn't surprised to see my answering machine blinking when I got home. Anna usually called on

Saturdays to see if I'd prefer doing something with her to drowning in my sorrow. I usually didn't. It had been the same exchange for months. She would ask if I was okay. I'd say yes—no sense in depressing her, too. Then she'd ask if I'd like to join her for lunch or dinner, depending on her plans with Dolen. I'd thank her and politely turn her down. She would argue, but I would insist that curling up on my sofa in front of the TV made me perfectly happy. She would moan, calling me an old lady and telling me that maybe I should rethink getting a cat. I'd tell her to have a nice weekend and then we'd hang up. I methodically kicked off my shoes near the front door and pressed the button to hear Anna's message—only it wasn't Anna.

It was Nick! He said he had a nice time at dinner and suggested we go to the movies. He said he couldn't wait to see me again! *Yes, yes, yes!* I was surprised he had called so soon. I looked in the mirror and winked at myself. *You can open up the stable doors, Julia. You can. You can ride again. You can love again.* My inner voice was uncharacteristically optimistic. She, like me, already knew Nick was thee one. I immediately called him back to accept his offer. Then I ripped off the tags from the new flowery sundress I had just gotten. I put it on and twirled around in front of my mirror admiring myself. I must've spent an hour deciding what color lipstick to wear and what perfume to spray on. I was in a hurry because I wanted to adorn my apartment with my purchases before he came to meet me. I danced around from room to room, singing along to *The Boxer* while I added the

finishing touches. *"I am older than I once was, and younger than I'll be, that's not unusual ~ It isn't strange after changes upon changes, we are more or less the same ~ After changes, we are more or less the same."*

Was I? Was I more or less the same, despite all that had happened in my life? I had scars, that was for sure, but I was still me and I was ready to move on. I was sure of it.

The movie was a comedy, but I appreciated listening to Nick laugh more than the movie itself. We got a large bag of salty, buttered popcorn to share, but he ate most of it. I had a kernel stuck between my teeth during half of the movie and all I could concentrate on was getting it out. When I finally did, I wanted no more popcorn. Could you imagine how romantic it would have been if Nick had leaned over to kiss me only to find a giant, mushy piece of popcorn kissing him back? Note to self: no more eating popcorn while on a date with the man of your dreams.

Nick *finally* put his arm across the back of my chair and turned his attention from the big screen to me.

"Are you enjoying the movie? You haven't laughed very much," he said.

I couldn't tell him that I had been too busy working out that damn piece of popcorn. That would've sounded classy. Instead I told him that I was having a great time, but that I didn't usually laugh out loud in theaters, which was the truth. He just smiled and nodded his head in understanding. Before the movie ended, I boldly placed my hand on his right knee. He never flinched, but rather responded by squeezing my shoulder. We were very comfortable with each other from the start. Like the true gentleman he was, he walked me home and said goodbye outside my building before hailing a cab.

"I'd love to do this again sometime," he said.

"How about next weekend?" I asked. There was no sense in waiting, no need for childish games, no sense in fighting it.

"I don't know if I can wait that long," he said grinning.

We stared into each other's eyes for what seemed like an eternity, then ever so slowly our lips moved toward one another's and locked in a beautiful never-ending kiss. I fought the urge to invite him in. We kissed for a second and a third time before I pulled away, saying goodnight before it was too late. I was stirring inside, secretly wanting him to ravish me.

We talked a couple times that following week, but we were both so busy that we didn't have the time to see each other even if we had wanted to. Friday night was the next time I saw him, exactly one week after our first date. He actually invited me to dinner at his place. He said he was going to make his mother's secret recipe for some fine Italian dish, but it was going to be a surprise. I picked up a bottle of red wine on my way home from the newspaper.

After I watered the plants, I got showered and dressed. I had already laid out a pair of white capri jeans and a red button-up shirt. I was very choosy with my undergarments, though. I habitually matched my bra and panties to my clothing, but I didn't want to wear plain old white and red seemed too daring. I went back and forth, back and forth and finally decided. What the hell. I wore the red.

Nick's apartment was much larger than mine and had a great view, but it wasn't very warm. His décor was contemporary, but unemotional. There were no pictures of friends or family, the lighting was harsh and the only greenery he had was plastic. His place was clean and neat, but I didn't expect differently since he mentioned having a housekeeper. There were gorgeous hardwood floors and black Italian leather furniture, but it all seemed so cold. Like a museum. You know, the you-can-look-but-you-can't-touch feeling. It had potential, but it lacked a woman's influence.

During one of our conversations that week, we had talked about our past relationships. Nick didn't say very much, but I learned that he had been engaged once before and had been hurt very badly. I didn't want to or need to know anymore, and likewise, I spared him all the ugly details about Tom. That was all in the past. This was now and for now we both were looking forward to getting to know each other better.

When I got close to the kitchen, I detected what smelled like marinara. Nick asked me to sit in the living room while he finished cooking. A copy of his book was lying on the coffee table and I picked it up and leafed through it again. Hmmm, an author. I was impressed. Restless, I walked around the room again. I noticed that my article for *The Times* had been framed and was hanging on the wall. Wow. What an expensive frame.

"Dinner's ready!" he called.

I sat at the dining room table and poured us each a glass of Cabernet. The music of Frank Sinatra was playing in the background as Nick served what looked like plain old spaghetti. I smiled in wonder and puzzlement recalling that the meal was supposed to be a secret family recipe.

"Okay, so it didn't turn out as planned," he confessed. "But I know how to make spaghetti!"

I just laughed and ate what I claimed to be the best spaghetti I had ever tasted. Honestly, it was pretty good. The sauce was a bit strong for my taste and I feared my breath would reek of garlic all night like Ed Garrison always did, but he added fresh mushrooms and my favorite—black olives. I was still impressed. You have to give a guy credit for trying. Besides, dinner wasn't the highlight of the evening, anyway. After we cleared the table, he refilled our wine glasses and led me to the balcony. With a remote control, he turned on the small outdoor speakers and we danced. It was Chicago. *"You know our love was meant to be, the kind of love to last forever..."* Right there, on the balcony of his forty-second floor apartment with the backdrop of the New York City skyline, we danced. *"And I want you here with me ~ from tonight, until the end of time..."* It was perfect. It was the most romantic night I had ever had. We danced closely and kissed passionately. It was as if our bodies were magnetic—pulling into each other, belonging as one. *"And I know ~ yes, I know that it's plain to see, we're so in love when we're together..."*

Just one look in his eyes and I knew. The eyes are the windows to the soul, you know. Without any words, Nick led me to his bedroom where we undressed each other and made love. *Yes, this is making love. Now I know. This is what it feels like to be in love.* He told me I was beautiful and that I intrigued him. He slowly unbuttoned my shirt and I held my breath as he kissed my neck. He slowly unfastened my jeans and simultaneously, I undid his belt buckle. We both stepped out of our pants and stood in front of each other, him in his boxers and me in my bra and panties. He caressed my bare shoulders and my arms, slowly, gently. We looked in each other's eyes and kissed again. We laid in his bed, side by side, touching each other and falling in love. We made love until four in the morning. It was intense and breathtaking. It wasn't wild or crazy, but it was sexy and it was real. The way it was supposed to be. Finally, we collapsed in each other's arms and slept until the late morning sun beat through the window and woke us up. It was almost eleven a.m. and it was already stuffy in the apartment. We could tell the day was going to be a scorcher.

CHAPTER EIGHT

We ate breakfast together that morning and nearly every Saturday morning after that for the next eight months. We were so in love with each other. He had been a lifelong resident of the city and was amused by my relentless fascination with all of it and laughed at my need to cross off each tourist attraction from my list. He acted like a tour guide, taking me to the Statue of Liberty and the Metropolitan Museum of Art.

Nick was perfect. Grandpa Joe would approve. I could hear him say, "You found a good one, baby girl." Boy did I miss him and my father. It was still hard to believe they were gone, even after all this time.

I told Nick all about them and shared my photo album with him early on in our relationship. I didn't realize how emotional I would be by simply looking at pictures of them and I cried so hard I was almost embarrassed, but Nick had comforted me ever so sweetly and it made me love him even more. Nick was the man I always dreamed I'd find. I was head over heels.

On Valentine's Day, we were at the top of the Empire State Building when Nick dropped to his knees and opened a box. No, it wasn't a ring—the box was too big and it was too soon. I looked at him skeptically as he gave me a key to his apartment and asked me to move in with him. I quickly grabbed the key from him, laughing hysterically. He knew exactly why. We were having dinner one night at a restaurant in Soho and we witnessed a wedding proposal. It was sweet, but I told him I didn't know why men did that. I told him I felt like an intruder, watching this momentous event of total strangers. I told him an engagement should be a private interaction and that if anyone ever asked me to marry them, it better not be in public. He joked that we may not be compatible after all because he had a soft spot for public declarations of love. This wasn't a proposal, but this was his humorous stab at proclaiming his affection for me.

We had spent many nights together since meeting last June, but we never discussed living together. It was totally unexpected, but it was the best present he could've given me. I wasn't quite sure how I felt about actually moving and giving up the independence I had for so long, but I was happy he asked. It meant he was serious enough about us to make such an important commitment. It did seem to be the next logical step, so I made the move slowly. My lease didn't end until May anyway, so that's when we combined the rest of our belongings. Making his place *our* place was relatively easy. Since we began dating, he had freshened up his apartment. He even had photos of us together scattered around. My favorite was the two of us at Central Park—an intimate side view of us kissing. Nick had taken it and it really captured the essence of how we were together. Carefree and loving.

We kept his furniture, but I insisted we get rid of the dismal gray rug so we replaced it with a bright one that had a pattern of geometric shapes and I brightened up the black couch with red tossed pillows. We both loved candles, so we put those everywhere. And the poor artificial plant had to go. I was no green thumb, but I could keep a plant alive. At least I thought I could. Well, make that a plant that doesn't require much care. Maybe a cactus.

Moving in with Nick proved to be a great decision. He was my best friend and I couldn't imagine life without him. He was everything I hoped for in a man. In a way, he reminded me of my father.

I hadn't heard from Gabe since December when I called to wish him a happy birthday, but I didn't dwell on it because my life was so fulfilled. Finding Nick really was the best thing that had ever happened to me. I guess New York wasn't so bad after all.

In June, on the one year anniversary of the day we first met, Nick asked me to go to a Yankees game. It wasn't my idea of a perfect anniversary date, but he was so excited about the ballgame so I reluctantly agreed. It's amazing how grown men can act little boys! I told him I'd only go if we could get peanuts and crackerjacks and he said that's exactly what he had in mind.

The Yankees were winning three to one in the bottom of the sixth when I looked at the lighted, animated board. It said, "Here we go, Yankees" and the crowd started chanting and clapping in sync.

Then, an unforgettable message scrolled across the screen.

"Julia,   WILL   YOU   MARRY   ME?
I'll   Love   You   Forever   &   Always,   Nick."

I was stunned. The fans were quiet and my eyes were wide as I looked from the board to my ever-so-adorable Nicholas. He was on his knee holding a gorgeous diamond ring. Although I thought it was cheesy, I was ecstatic. I glanced at the board to see myself and Nick televised. I sighed, remembering the talk where I told him I hated this kind of commercialized, unoriginal public displays of affection. But I couldn't stop smiling. I knew he did this as a direct result of my aversion to it, which made me smile even more.

"Julia, you are my sun and moon, my heart and soul. Will you marry me, my love?" he asked, his voice wavering. Tears of joy welled up in my eyes.

"Yes!" I shouted. "Yes, yes!"

The stadium went wild with excitement, not over the game, but for us. Even the ball players looked up at us. It was the best seventh-inning stretch ever. It was the most wonderful moment of my life. I was overwhelmed with delight.

"Oh, Nick!" I jumped up and grabbed him around the chest and held him as tight as I could. I was deliriously happy. I never wanted the day to end. I never wanted our love to end. I never wanted to wake up to a day without him.

That night we made love. It was slow and methodical. Nick softly caressed me, tracing over the curves of my body. He kissed every inch of my body and soon, slowly and gently, he made his way inside of me. It was heavenly. He was looking at me with complete admiration and an unspoken devotion. As our bodies rocked back and forth, our eyes remained locked. We were fixated on each other. He really loved me; I could feel it. There was an emotional connection that was so strong, it brought me to tears. I was raw with emotion. There was an implied trust, a trust that was so deep and so momentous. I realized then that the difference between making love and simply having sex came down to trust—something I never felt before. It was magical. Our bodies moved together rhythmically. We stayed in constant eye contact until we climaxed—first him, then me. My body shuddered underneath him, tears running down my cheeks.

Who knew a love of this magnitude and this intensity even existed? I wouldn't have believed it if I hadn't been so fortunate to find it. It was like all my lucky stars gathered to bring us together. Oh how lucky I was.

*　　*　　*　　*　　*　　*　　*　　*　　*　　*　　*

Our engagement lasted a little longer than a year and we got married the next September. The wedding was small, but elegant. I couldn't help wishing my father could have been there to walk me down the aisle. Unbeknownst to me, Nick had asked my trusty old friend Gabe to do the honor. I had called Gabe a few weeks after Nick's proposal and he said he was happy for me, but I didn't know if it was genuine or obligatory. I hadn't planned on even inviting him to the wedding, but Nick thought it would be a nice surprise, and it was. The guest list was short. I didn't have any relatives and Nick's family was small. Anna was my maid of honor, of course, and Dolen and Ross were there. Nick's best man was a longtime friend of his from college who was very good looking, but he apparently wasn't marriage material, according to Nick's mother. He had been married and divorced twice already and joked about it during his toast to us.

And I can't forget Gabe's girlfriend Cara. When I saw the two of them together, something seemed off. I couldn't put my finger on it, but my instincts told me she wasn't right for him. I wanted Gabe to have what I did with Nick, but Cara just didn't fit my ideal. She was yappy and her voice was nasally. She reminded me of a little pesky dog like a Chihuahua or a Pomeranian. Yeah, more like a Pomeranian.

Anyway, the day was picturesque. It was sunny and warm. There were a few clouds, but the sky was bright blue. I felt as if the heavens were shining down on me. The ceremony was brief and emotional. Nick was beyond perfect. I was so lucky and so in love.

We had a grand time at the reception. It was held in a hotel ballroom where guests were treated to lobster, shrimp and caviar. The food was spectacular — except for those horrible fish eggs that Nick drooled over — and the band was phenomenal. They played until our feet ached. Our first dance as husband and wife mirrored our first dance on his balcony, only this time we weren't alone. He held me close while the band sang Chicago's song. *"Baby, you're the meaning in my life. You're the inspiration. You bring feeling to my life. You're the inspiration..."* I rested my head on his chest and looked up to see tears in his eyes.

"I love you, Julia," he said and twirled me, then instantly pulled me back into him.

Then he sang along, softly in my ear, for only me to hear. *"Wanna have you near me, I wanna have you hear me sayin' ~ No one needs you more than I need you."*

Nick and I stayed at the hotel that night, then left the next morning for our honeymoon. Our first night as husband and wife was just as I dreamed it would be. It was as if we were making love for the first time — our bodies empowered by passion and tenderness.

I once read somewhere that ninety-four percent of people believed they had a soulmate. I had apparently been one of those elite six percent who thought it was bogus. That is, until I met Nick. I felt as if we were destined to be together. It sounds lame to say it must've been written in the stars, but being in love makes you think of all those old clichés — the kind Grandpa Joe used so often.

Our honeymoon was heavenly. A week of pure bliss. I wanted to go to San Francisco and he didn't want to budge from the Bahamas, but we compromised and decided on Porta Vallarta, Mexico. It was beautiful there. We swam and danced and drank and you can imagine what else. The beaches were absolutely majestic. The sand was white and the water a crystal clear blue. We took early morning walks on the shore and evening dips in the ocean's warm waters. I snorkeled for the first time, swam with dolphins and partook in a baby sea turtle release at our resort. It was something I'd never forget. I loved turtles and it felt so noble to be a part of an effort to preserve the endangered animals. Nick and I and a small group of hotel guests were shown the proper way to handle the turtle before releasing it. We were to hold it between our right thumb and forefinger, resting it gently in the palm of our left hand. I did as we were told and was amazed by the tiny turtle's powerful front flippers that strained forcefully against my hand in an instinctive attempt to reach the ocean. It tickled. I watched the struggling creature and said a silent prayer that she would make it even though the odds were against her. As instructed, I released the baby turtle and watched as she made her way to the sea. She crawled quickly toward the water, stumbled a bit when she reached the edge but continued on, willful and strong. Just like me. The little turtle had many challenges ahead, but as long as she didn't give up, she'd make it. I was sure of it.

Our vacation from the real world ended all too soon. As much as I loved our city life together, I was saddened by the idea of returning to it. Nick assured me that we would visit Mexico again someday. Life became somewhat normal again back in the Big Apple. I went back to the chaotic environment of the newspaper after my two weeks of paradise and Nick dove headfirst into the research he had put on hold.

Part of the reason I think we loved each other so much was that we admired one another. At the end of my work day, I frequently stopped at his office before heading home just to watch him work. I was so in awe of him. And a day didn't pass without him reading *The New York Times*. We were perfect for each other. Spending every waking moment with him would have made me the happiest woman in the world, but life disrupts that, of course and the time we had together was often interrupted by work and his frequent business trips. I hated it when he went away. Not because I didn't trust him. No, he was the most faithful, most loyal man I ever knew. But I missed him terribly. The first weekend we spent apart I felt as if there wasn't enough air to fill my lungs. I couldn't breathe comfortably. I couldn't eat. I couldn't sleep. I told myself that it was ridiculous. I mean, he'd be home in a couple days for goodness sake, but I couldn't help it. I didn't feel whole without him. Why was love so suffocating sometimes?

Gabe once told me he thought the definition of love was when every single song you hear seems to have something to do with that special someone in your life. But I knew it was much more than that— much. I ached for Nick when he wasn't near me. I longed to hear his voice. Time spent without him was agonizing. Was a love life like this healthy or danger-ous? I had no rational control over the way he made me feel. All I knew is that with ties as strong as ours, they'd never be broken.

Anna and Dolen got married almost a year after Nick and I did. She was the best girlfriend I ever had, although she was my polar opposite and sometimes made no sense at all. While she was trying on wed-ding gowns at a boutique in midtown, her ex-husband and his new fiancé walked in. What were the chances? It was an awkward moment and I couldn't believe that even the largest of cities can suddenly seem crowded. Anna froze and stared at both of them with fire in her eyes.

"Oh Lord and Behold," she finally said. "Look who it is."

"Forget about them," I told her, contemplating for a second if she meant to say 'low and behold.' I just shook my head. Who knew with her. She never got idioms right.

"You should be thanking what's-his-name," I told her. "You never would've met Dolen if he had been faithful."

"You're right," she said as we walked out of the store. "I just didn't know whether to shit, faint, wind my watch or go to the movies."

I just looked at her. What do you say to that? It was ridiculous and nonsensical, but that was Anna.

CHAPTER NINE

Nick and I had been married for two years when we discussed having a baby. We both had demanding careers that fulfilled us, but life didn't seem worth anything without children. What was the point of being successful if you had nobody with whom to share it? We talked about it a lot, often at bedtime and into the wee hours of the morning. I didn't know if I was ready yet, though. I think he wanted a child more than I did, at least at first. I questioned myself for not being as enthusiastic as he was. I guess I was being selfish. I was already content, so why rock the boat? I knew all too well that expecting too much happiness usually backfired.

We decided to drop the debate and just see what happened. As much as I loved Nick, sex with him wasn't sensational. Nick was an emotional lover. To him, sex was very private and wholesome. He wasn't into quickies or outdoor rendezvous. He didn't desire to try anything kinky and would blush at the mere mention of anything carnal. He liked it straightforward, usually missionary style. I always had a wild streak and enjoyed sex in all it had to offer — sometimes gentle, sometimes rough, sometimes slow and sometimes fast, sometimes with a complete stranger just when the mood would strike. But I never wanted Nick to see that side of me, so I kept my sexual desires as low-key as I could. My inner voice told me that it wasn't a good idea to not be up front with Nick about my true sensuality. *You'll get bored*, she had said. *Then you'll end up leaving him just like your mother left your father.* But I ignored her. There was so much more to a marriage than just sexual satisfaction. I'll admit, it was a little boring at times, but it was who he was and sex with him was still satisfying because of the deep emotional connection we shared during intercourse.

So although it got a little monotonous, we tried and tried and tried. On one night in particular, I had a good feeling about getting pregnant. It was the right time of the month. The mood was perfect. Nick had just come home from his nightly three-mile jog. With his face flushed and his hair ruffled, he looked so incredibly sexy that he took my breath away. I didn't care that he was soaked with perspiration. The way the sweat was glistening on his strong forearms was such a turn on that I wanted him right then and there. My heart was pounding with anticipation and my eyes transfixed on his masculine body. The rest goes without saying. I felt closer to him than ever before. I don't know if it was because we were trying to make a baby, but he turned me on and on and on.

Obviously to no avail. I was utterly disappointed when I woke up one morning to discover that I had gotten my period. What could we be doing wrong? I scheduled an appointment with my doctor, but it wasn't very helpful.

"Sometimes, Julia, it takes quite a while after you stop taking the pill," was all she said and urged me to be patient and keep trying. *Easy for her to say*, I thought as I smirked at the picture on her desk of three adorable kids.

Ten months went by, and still, nothing. I was beginning to worry. Although I wasn't sure if I was ready when we first talked about it, I was more than ready now. I don't know if it was my internal clock pressuring me or my yearning to please Nick, but my need for a baby had become an obsession. I'd wonder constantly—was this time successful? Do I have a baby growing inside of me? Will I finally be a mother? The wait was agonizing, the anxiety immeasurable and the stress immense. And I kept it all to myself for fear that speaking about it may jinx my chances. My body was changing, too, for some ungodly reason. My periods had become irregular, wickedly tricking me each time I was late. At first I attributed it to my body adjusting to the absence of the birth control pills I had taken for so long, but it was more than that. I was also experiencing sharp pains in my abdomen and a dull, relentless pain in my lower back. I was afraid to tell Nick, but I knew I had to and I was glad when I finally did. He was a saint, as usual, assuring me that we'd figure it out together and coaxing me to go see my doctor.

After many tests, I found out I had cysts on my ovaries. That didn't sound so bad. But it wasn't good news. My doctor said I had a twenty-percent chance of ever being able to have children. I couldn't help feeling sorry for myself. It hit me hard, but we kept trying. Twenty percent wasn't great, but it was better than no chance at all, I told myself. I read anything and everything I could get my hands on about conceiving. I knew my most fertile times, the best position—yes, Nick's usual—and what vitamins to take. I even knew that I should be drinking green tea and taking baby aspirin daily. I also took evening primrose oil each day and a teaspoon of cough syrup at night. No, I didn't have a cold, but it was supposed to thin my cervical mucus, I guess. See, I knew it all. Still, it wasn't enough. After seven more months of negative pregnancy tests, I felt like such a failure. Not being able to have children had thus far been one of life's most devastating disappointments. I constantly asked myself why, but I had no answers. I questioned my purpose in the world. What is the point of life if one can't pass on experiences, memories, precious treasures? Again, no answer.

A baby encounter was always a struggle. I held

my belly, unconsciously, as I looked at women with their precious babies. I'd listen to an expectant mother carry on giddily over baby names and nursery décor and a sharp pang of jealousy would urge me not to congratulate her. But I did. It was expected, even if I did so with a meaningless smile from an empty soul and a broken heart. Was I blessed with motherly instincts or cursed? I knew other women at work that had absolutely no desire to have children. I'm not sure I could ever relate to them. I had always loved children. Even though I didn't have a mother as a role model, I always pictured myself as a mom, like Gabe's mom—warm and caring, baking chocolate chip cookies and kissing boo-boos. I couldn't help but to think that I'd be a good mom. Of course, it's easy to say that when you know you may never be one. The deep sorrow inside me and the longing for that which I could not have threatened to destroy me. The possibility of not bearing a child was a haunting reality and one only a woman in my position could understand. Nick didn't understand either. Although he wanted a child, he said he'd be okay without one, too. He would lovingly say that we'd still have a great life without kids—that we would travel more. But really, I knew it was a great disappointment for him as well. He was good with children, too, which made me feel even worse.

Once we were at a friend's party and one of the women had brought her baby. Nick held the baby boy, tickled him and made him coo. He turned to the woman and asked her if she'd have another one and give it to us. He said it jokingly and I laughed along with everyone else, but inside I was crushed.

Trying to become pregnant nearly ruined my career and put a tremendous strain on my relationship with Nick. I was obsessed with having a baby. Baby lust is what Anna called it. I knew it was irrational. I had thought about the sleep deprivation, the tremendous responsibility, the loss of freedom, the stretch marks. But I didn't care. Can anyone truly understand the depth of baby fever? It's not a fleeting sensation. It was an uncontrollable desire that was eating at me from the inside out.

I was successful in most everything I did and I was having a very difficult time accepting that this was out of my control. I mean a dog can have babies, why can't I? Frustration, pain, the sense of personal inadequacy, while at the same time the world rubs it in. Pregnant women everywhere I turned. Without a baby, wanting a baby, you stand outside the window of the candy store, drooling.

Then the worst news of all—Gabe was going to be a father. I know I should have been happy for him, but I wasn't. For the first time, I was envious of him and Cara. I already didn't like her and this was even more reason to loathe her. Why was she able to get pregnant and I wasn't? Just what the world needed—another Pomeranian. At least he still cared enough about me to call me with his news.

"So are you and Cara getting married?" I thought I already knew the answer, but I asked anyway. Gabe always stepped up to the plate when it counted—even with responsibilities that weren't his own. One time in college I had been a bit careless with a one-night stand

and nearly went insane worrying about being pregnant. I was crying on his shoulder imagining raising a baby alone. Gabe told me not to fear because he loved me enough to marry me and care for the baby as his own. It was the sweetest thing he had ever said to me. I wiped away my tears and stood there, staring at him with admiration.

"You really are the greatest friend a girl could have, Gabriel Jones," I had told him. It was, of course, a false alarm, but his devotion to me tugged at my heart deep inside, and feelings I'd never admit to tried to surface. I hid them well, ignoring them and refusing to acknowledge them until they went away.

"Not right away," he answered surprisingly.

"What?" I was shaken back to the present.

"We're not getting married. It's too much right now. We're waiting until after the baby comes," *Ouch.* There goes one of those pangs of jealousy I told you about. Like a knife, piercing my heart.

Then I asked the ultimate question. The one I'd been wondering about since the first time I saw the two of them together in his driveway.

"Are you in love with her, Gabe?" I just had to hear it to believe it.

"Oh JC, what's love anyway?" I was suddenly sad for him. He obviously wasn't in love if he answered that way. Don't get me wrong. I didn't think Cara was the one for him, but I had hoped she was now that she was having his baby.

We agreed to keep in touch more often and he said he'd call with baby updates. I never mentioned my own battle with infertility to him. I didn't want to rain on his parade. And knowing Gabe, he would've been concerned about being insensitive and hurting me, so he'd probably just avoid it by not calling me again and I didn't want that to happen. I enjoyed our periodic conversations. He was a part of me and a piece of home that I never wanted to let go.

When I hung up, I selfishly cried. Well, it was really more like a wail. I pitied myself and I was angry. Angry that Cara and all the other Caras in the world were able to have babies and I wasn't. *Why???* I screamed to nobody at all. *Why can't I have a baby?* I was mad at everyone. Hearing the word *adopt* made me cringe. Hasn't everyone seen the Lifetime movies where the woman's baby is eventually ripped out of her arms and her life by the birth mother who suddenly changes her mind? No, that wasn't for me. I couldn't survive that kind of heartache. I saw red when Nick's mother said that "children aren't for everybody." I wanted to reach out and slug someone, but who? Whose fault was it? Was it mine? It must have been. Nobody else could be to blame. So I turned against myself. I was disgusted when I looked in the mirror. *What did you do to deserve this? What did you do?* I yelled at my reflection like a madwoman, a lunatic. Anna told me that I had become so bitter it was scaring her. Truthfully, I was scaring myself. The day Nick found me slumped in the corner of our bedroom holding onto the music box my father had given me with a death grip was the day I knew I needed help. I had hit rock bottom. I had been pathetically listening to Braham's Lullaby for hours. My eyes were puffy and my cheeks were streaked with mascara. It was not one of my shining moments. If the meaning of insanity is repeatedly doing something you *know* is insane, then I really had gone crazy. The next day I enrolled in a support program for women experiencing infertility issues. Once I let go of the anger and resentment toward my body, I was able to start trying again without being obsessed. I learned that stress only works against you when you're trying to conceive. I went to a specialist who prescribed me a drug to induce ovulation. It made me terribly sick, but that didn't stop me from taking it. It was worth it. At least I had been given hope and for once, that hope wasn't false.

In May, just days after I turned 32, I heard the words I had been waiting so long to hear. I was pregnant! A tremendous joy filled my heart. I finally felt like a woman—a real woman. Ecstatic, I went straight from the doctor's office to the nearest baby store and bought an adorable, incredibly tiny bib that said "Daddy's Little Angel" on it. I had it giftwrapped in a subtle pastel blue paper with an iridescent bow. Nick wouldn't know what to expect. I wanted him to be as surprised and thrilled as I was. As soon as he walked in the door and set down his bag, I thrust the gift toward him.

"Open it!" I gushed enthusiastically.

He didn't let me down. He was literally floored. He dropped to his knees, hugging my legs and resting his head on my stomach.

"Hi little one," he said patting my belly. His reaction was just what I dreamed it would be. He was going to be a perfect father, I thought as I looked down at him. I felt like the luckiest woman alive. I only wished I could have shared the good news with my own father.

"Let's celebrate!" He jumped up excitedly. "We'll get something to eat—you're probably starving—and we should buy something for the baby and then stop for hot fudge sundaes with whipped cream and extra nuts!" He was even happier than I imagined him to be. I laughed at his fervor and grabbed my jacket.

Nick and I loved each other immensely and having a baby seemed to intensify our relationship. We had so much fun together. He wanted to partake in everything, from ultrasound appointments to painting the nursery. Anna said she was green with envy. She said that she didn't know of many men who would be so doting and so involved. I agreed that I must have found that one-in-a-million guy. And how grateful I was that I did. Before Nick, I had been fairly independent, but now I needed him. All of my happiness was wrapped up in him. If I didn't have him, I didn't want anything. He was my love, my life.

Our baby girl arrived nine months later, right on time. She was born on the tenth of February in one of the coldest New York winters ever. It didn't matter to us, though. We were overjoyed. The delivery went well and our newborn was perfect—ten little fingers and ten tiny toes and very strong lungs, that was for sure. And she was the most beautiful baby I had ever seen. Camden Jessica Stanton—an extension of the love Nick and I shared, a perfect little angel.

I remember holding her for the first time. She was so tiny, so fragile. I was extra careful with her and begged the nurses not to take her away, but they said I needed some rest and I guess they were right. I was exhausted and fell asleep as soon as I shut my eyes. That night I dreamt the most wonderful dream. To tell you about it would only denigrate its relevance, so I'll keep it to myself.

When we brought Camden home, our family felt complete. My own family. Nick surprised me with a charming old rocking chair in the nursery. It, like he, was absolutely perfect. I felt so blessed.

Life changed dramatically with our new addition, but definitely for the better. Camden was a healthy infant and she quickly became a curious child. She was extremely active and rather restless. As she began to crawl, I could barely keep up with her. At first I doubted myself. I was worried I wouldn't be a good mom, but I soon discovered that motherhood is learned along the way. It doesn't matter how many books you read or how much advice you get from your mother-in-law. It can be trying at times, but the rewards are plentiful. Despite the lack of sleep, I wouldn't have changed it for the world. I loved being a mommy and Nick loved being a dad. He sure was a wonderful father. He took turns with nightly feedings, changed his share of dirty diapers and sang the sweetest lullabies. He hated leaving in the mornings, but as soon as he would get home from work, he'd scoop up Camden in his arms, holding her high above his head and telling her he'd give her the moon if he could. Then he'd smother her with kisses and tickle her and she'd laugh the cutest laugh you ever heard. We were so incredibly happy—the kind that made you want to puke, the kind I thought only existed in fairytales, the kind you know is too good to be true.

And it was—too good to be true, that is. Experience has cruelly taught me that all good things come to an end. Why, I'll never know. Why we're teased with simplicity and taunted by delusions of grandeur will always remain a mystery. Call it fate, call it destiny, call it what you will. I call it life. Life in all of its infamous glory. Life with all it has to offer and even more it has to take away.

CHAPTER TEN

It was the day before my birthday — September 11th. Before Nick left for work that morning, I had prepared him breakfast in the nude. No, not bacon! I didn't cook naked often, okay never, but he had been joking about it the night before and Camden was still sleeping, so why not? I had to spice things up every once in a while.

He laughed as he walked into the kitchen and saw me there, spreading cream cheese on his bagel.

"Gotta love me," I said and served him his gourmet breakfast.

"It's not that hard to do," he answered and kissed my neck.

"Wish we had more time," he said as he winked and sat there with his bagel and coffee, looking me up and down. Then we kissed goodbye and he headed out on his way to his office on Barclay Street, a block from the World Trade Center. I woke up Camden, got her ready and dropped her off at the daycare center on my way to *The Times*.

Less than an hour later, I was sitting at my desk in Times Square when the first reports came flooding in of a hijacked plane deliberately crashing into one of the Twin Towers. At first it appeared to be an accident. My heart was suddenly heavy. The whole office got quiet. We were all centered around a lone television set, our hearts racing with fear. What in the world was happening? I looked at the clock. It was 8:48 a.m. The first live televised report just came on. There was black smoke coming from the North Tower. Thick, charcoal-gray smoke escalated from gaping holes in the side of the building. Before I even had time to react, a second plane crashed into the south tower, creating a fireball of smoke and flames. A powerful shockwave traveled down to the ground and back up again, shaking the building. The TV station's satellite feed froze on the image of the second impact. I screamed out in dismay! Tears welled up in my eyes. *My God*, I thought, *where's Nick?* He walked in front of the Twin Towers every day en route to his office. My heart was pounding with anticipation and fear. What would happen next? It seemed as if the world were ending. The FAA was banning all takeoffs nationwide for flights coming into or going through New York airspace and they were closing all NYC airports. All the bridges and tunnels into Manhattan were closed. *What in God's name is going on?!* I frantically called Nick's cell phone, but he didn't answer. I looked at my watch. 9:25 a.m. It was already being called a terrorist attack even before the next hit came—on the Pentagon in Washington, D.C., collapsing one side of the structure. This was an overwhelming catastrophe.

Anna and I were supposed to be working on stories related to the mayoral primary election, which was taking place that day. It was supposed to be a normal day like every other. I called Nick again, but it went to voicemail. Maybe he was in a meeting. *Please be safe, please be in a meeting.* It was Tuesday. Yes, of course—he always had meetings on Tuesday mornings. Still, I felt like I couldn't breathe. I ran from the office with Anna and many other coworkers and we watched in disbelief at the big screen in Times Square as the South Tower came tumbling down. Monstrous, billowing clouds of smog and debris pushed their way through the streets of New York City. Silently, we stared at the giant screen in awe. We were stunned. Anna fumbled in her bag for her inhaler and took two huge puffs. My editor, Ed Garrison, started barking out orders right there on the street, but nobody listened. We were all in shock at the absolute devastation unfolding before us. I tried to call Nick again. Again, voicemail. I fought back the tears as an intense sadness washed over me. I wasn't alone in my sorrow and woe. A melancholy lingered over the city.

About thirty minutes later, the North Tower

buckled and fell to its demise. It was like a scene from a Hollywood movie. My body felt like a ton of bricks. I couldn't move. I could barely pull myself from the screen. I didn't want to panic, but I felt an unsettling fear rise up in my throat. *Stay calm*, I told myself. *Just breathe and stay calm.* The city was in a state of chaos. Hundreds of firefighters, police and rescue workers were rushing to the scene. I said a silent prayer for all of them, thinking of my father.

My mind instantly went to Camden. I called the daycare center, but couldn't get through. She was only a few blocks away, not anywhere near the World Trade Center, but I needed to know that she was safe. I ran there, in my heels, as quickly as I could. I don't remember getting there, my mind was racing faster than my legs. *Oh thank God, she was safe.* I was relieved to see her playing with blocks, without a care in the world, totally unaware of the tremendous turmoil unfolding all around us. I snatched her up and held her close to me.

"I love you baby girl," I whispered in her ear. "Mommy loves you so much." A tear rolled down my cheek. The love I had for Camden was like no other. I had an unexplained protective instinct for her from the moment she was born and a love that I knew would always be unconditional. Having a child caused me to revisit my thoughts about my own mother. I would never understand a woman like her, abandoning her child. I couldn't stand the idea of leaving my baby at daycare on a day like this, let alone walking out the door and never planning to return. I didn't want her out of my sight. I wanted to take her home, but on second thought, she was just as safe right where she was, so I kissed her goodbye, told her mommy would see her later and went back to my job. What else could I do?

I grabbed my notebook and headed to the scene, as instructed, to get a story. From blocks away, I could smell it. A toxic smell like from an electrical fire. When I saw the devastation up close, I was floored. Who could have done this and why? *My God, why?* How many deaths would there be? How many survivors?

I saw a black dress shoe lying amidst a pile of rubber and instinctively picked it up and looked at the size. Ten. I breathed a sigh of relief—it wasn't Nick's. I knew I had to stay a safe distance away from the fallen structures, but I couldn't tell how close I was because the air was thick with grayish-black smoke. I coughed, choking on the dirty air. My breathing was labored as I ran around, looking for someone who could give me some information to print. The streets looked war-sticken. I couldn't believe what I saw. I pinched myself in hopes that I was having a nightmare. I wasn't.

I thought about how handsome Nick looked before he left that morning. He was dressed smartly in a pin-striped suit. I frantically called his cell for the umpteenth time. *Please Nick, please answer your phone. Please be okay. I need you. I love you.* My heart ached for the families of the victims. So many people had left their homes that morning, thinking like we did, that they were just off to another day of work and would be sitting at their dinner table later that evening with their loved ones. A dark cloud came over my heart. The ash was falling from the sky like snow. It fell into my hair and onto my shoulders, but I didn't care. I wiped it from my face. There was mass destruction all around me. It was Mayhem. I was in a whirlwind of terror. I yelled Nick's name, calling for him, hoping against hope that he'd hear me. How silly. I needed to stop worrying. He was probably fine and helping out in any way he could. It was what he did. It was one of his greatest assets and greatest faults. When we were dating, he stepped in front of a man wielding a knife on the subway and talked him into handing it over. I remember being terrified as I listened to Nick reason with the troubled young man. He handed Nick his weapon without incident and the other passengers applauded the both of them. When we stopped, Nick walked out with his arms around the man's shoulder so compassionately and talked with the police officer who was taking the man into custody.

When we were on our honeymoon, he had risked his own life to save a stranger from drowning. While part of me was proud of him for his compulsion to help others in danger, part of me resented him for it too. It was both admirable and stupid. How could he risk not seeing me or Camden again? I know he felt invincible and he often forgot just how fragile life really is—his, that is. *My Nick, everyone's hero, where are you now?* I tried to concentrate on my story. It wasn't hard to find someone who had one—everybody did. Still, I scoured the streets looking for someone I knew, someone that might know where Nick was. It was impossible. People were scattered everywhere. While the emergency crews ran in one direction, people ran in the other. Hundreds were fleeing the city on foot because no transportation was coming in or going out. Even the subways were closed. It was pandemonium. *God, have mercy on us all.* The city would never be the same again. I stopped beside a television reporter to hear what he was saying. He called this day the Pearl Harbor of the twenty-first century. "The worst terrorist attack in world history," he said. How could this have happened and who did it? When would this be over? There were so many unanswered questions. I interviewed about a dozen people, but their reactions were all relatively the same—shock, fear, sadness, anger, disbelief. I called Nick again, several times to no avail. The morning had begun so beautifully and ended in tragedy. This day would be unforgettable. The nation was surprisingly vulnerable. The scene—ghastly and overwhelming. The number of those unaccounted for—staggering. The destruction—appalling. It all seemed so senseless. America was under fire and all I could do was pray—for those whose lives were lost, for those who were injured, for families of those who had died, for Nick. I forced myself to avoid thinking the worst. He would be okay. He had to be.

It was 5:20 p.m. I was just blocks away when 7 World Trade Center, a forty-seven-story building collapsed. I had still heard nothing from Nick. I looked at my watch again. 7 p.m. I was in a daze. Where did the past hour go? I don't think I had moved from where I was the hour before. The daylight quickly disappeared. The night was eerie as rescuers sifted through debris. I had made arrangements for Anna to pick up Camden and keep her for the night until I found Nick.

Volunteers were searching for survivors. I joined them, combing the streets for any sign of life amidst the rubble, until I was asked to stay back from the "crime scene," the officer called it. I flashed my media badge and he said he was sorry, but it just wasn't safe. I told him I couldn't find my husband, that he wasn't answering his cell, but he urged me to go home muttering that communication was sketchy all over the city. I was helpless and exhausted, so I complied and went home.

When I got to our apartment, I was disheartened to find it empty. It was quiet—way too quiet. I ran to the blinking light on the answering machine. The only messages were from Gabe, urging me to call, saying he was worried about me. I turned on the news just in time to catch the president addressing the nation. It was 8:30 p.m.

I was beside myself. What to do, what to do. I grabbed a picture frame out of my bedroom and ripped out the photo of me and Nick. Then I went back to where I had been, clutching the photo against my chest. It was all I had. *Please, dear God, don't let this be all I have a left of him—a photo, an intangible reminder of his gentle smile, his smooth cheeks, his brown eyes, the freckle on the bridge of his nose.* I was scared and starting to become hysterical. My head was spinning with emotions—swirling with memories. I thought about breakfast that morning. I could still see Nick's sly smile when he sat down at the table and opened the newspaper, pretending not to notice that I didn't have any clothes on. My last words to him replayed in my mind. *Gotta love me, gotta love me, gotta love me...* A passage from the book *Dante's Inferno* came rushing back to me like a ton of bricks: "There is no greater grief than the misery of recalling happier times."

"Nick! For God's sake, where are you?!" I cried out in pain and in fury. I wanted to lash out, to retaliate. *Why was this happening? Dear Lord, can you hear me? Why? Why?*

"Why?!" I yelled, falling to my knees. My hair was plastered to my forehead from crying and there were black streaks of mascara streaming down my face, but none of that was important now. He had to be somewhere—he had to be alive.

I finally headed to Bellevue Hospital, asking if anybody had seen him. Then I went to Saint Vincent's. My heart raced against hope. There was a list of people who had been treated or admitted, but his name wasn't on it. Still, I walked around showing his picture to strangers, asking if he had been there. Nothing. It was almost eleven o'clock and I still hadn't heard from him. I was physically and psychologically drained. *Nick, where are you?* I now feared that he was hurt, or worse. I must've said at least a hundred prayers. *Please dear God, bring him home to me. What will I do without him? Help me find him, please Lord, help me.* I walked around in a fog, grief stricken. *Where could he be? God, are you there?* The country had been maliciously attacked and the father of my baby was missing. I felt lost, empty, like a shell. *I have to find him, I have to find him, I have to find him.* And I wasn't stopping until I did. It was after midnight when I decided to go back to Bellevue. After midnight—that meant it was my birthday. I had always thought my seventh birthday was the worst one of my life, until now.

"Has anybody seen this man?" I asked repeatedly.

"Excuse me," I said to a group of doctors who were taking a coffee break. "Do any of you remember treating this man?" I pointed to the picture of my ever-so-devoted husband. They all shook their heads. The lump in my throat got bigger. Discouraged, I turned around and started to leave, but something urged me to stay. My hands were shaking as I once again held up our wedding photo and walked down the hallway, asking if anybody had seen Nick.

"I did," someone said in a quiet, feeble voice. I thought I must have imagined it until she spoke again. "He saved my son," she said looking at my photograph. She was a young Hispanic woman. She was covered in soot and her blouse was torn. She had a small cut above her eye and the blood had dried in a zigzag pattern down the side of her face.

"Are you sure?" I asked her.

"Yes," she answered confidently. "I will never forget his face. The face of an angel."

"Do you know where he is?" There were tears in my eyes, listening to her describe the way Nick had come just in time and rescued her little boy. She said she was praying for a miracle and that Nick was heaven sent.

"He's in there," she said and pointed to the emergency room doors.

"Thank you," I called behind me as I rushed in that direction.

"No, thank you!" She called to me.

I was about to walk through the doors but was stopped by a nurse.

"I think my husband's here," I told her impatiently and showed her his picture.

"What's his name?" she asked,

"Nicholas Stanton."

The place was a zoo. I figured she wouldn't be able to recognize a face, let alone a name.

"I think he's in the O-R," she said. "Wait here."

Oh God, I prayed, *please let him be okay. Please, please, please.*

"Ma'am," she shook me from my prayers. "He is in the operating room. He has suffered a crush injury to his chest and his lung collapsed. We don't yet know the full extent of the internal damage. You need to sit down over here and the doctor will see you as soon as he can."

The wait was agonizing. What had happened? How serious was his injury? When would he be coming home? As I sat in the makeshift waiting room, I was so wracked with fear I couldn't stop shaking. I anxiously glanced at the clock about a hundred times before I stood up and paced the room. My knuckles were so tightly clenched they were white and my face was pale and emotionless. A thousand thoughts entered my mind, but I just couldn't face the harsh possibility that he might not make it. I refused to. I was instantly dizzy and nauseated. I felt faint, so I sat back down and reassured myself that everything would be okay.

Soon I would be holding Nick's hand in mine and never let it go. I'd be his lifeline, keeping vigil until he returned home. Soon I would kiss his cheek and tell him I love him now and forever. Soon. Soon.

The doors opened and I immediately stood up in anticipation. The surgeon walked in and I knew. My knees weakened and my heart sunk to the depths of my stomach. I barely heard him say the words. The room was spinning, his voice was muffled and distant. The moment was surreal. I grasped my throat, choking on my own sorrow before I fell to the floor screaming for myself to wake up, begging for the inevitable not to be real.

"No-o-o-o-o! Not my Nick. Oh God, no!" I sobbed uncontrollably for what seemed like an eternity before I had no more tears to cry. Then I sat expressionless and silent—half in shock, half in denial. It took mere minutes before the reality set in.

"Why-y-y-y-y?" I screamed. "Why?" What kind of God would let this happen? Why was life so cruel? My only true love was ripped from my life without warning, without saying goodbye.

How could I go on? How could I walk? How could I write? How could I breathe? How was I going to live without him? If it hadn't been for my daughter, I would have gone home and drugged myself into a permanent sleep, but she needed me. Poor baby. She just lost her father and didn't even know it. I had to control myself for her. But how in God's name was I going to tell her that daddy wouldn't be coming home? How could I shatter her world as mine had just been?

Damn you, Nick. Damn you for loving me like nobody ever had. Damn you for leaving me.

CHAPTER ELEVEN

I didn't eat. I didn't sleep. I existed—if you could call it that. All alone. That's how I felt. Who cared if I lived or died—except Camden of course. Oh, my poor baby. If only I could hold it together for her, but I couldn't. I never thought I'd ever feel that life just wasn't worth living, but I did.

Dear God, fill my soul with something worthwhile. Life isn't LIFE without him. I was depressed and there was no way of bringing me back. *Just leave me be.* I lost hope. I lost faith. I even questioned God's existence. How could He have let this happen? Didn't He ever hear me? When those thoughts kept popping into my head, I knew I was doomed. The Julia I used to know would say that everything happens for a reason, even the fire. The Julia I used to know could pull it together when times were rough. The Julia I used to know wasn't easily defeated — especially by herself.

I turned to my sweet friend Bloody Mary. Did I become and alcoholic? No. Just a few drinks to erase the painful memories, just a few drinks to help me cope. I guess that's what every alcoholic says, but really, I was still in control — of the drinking, that is.

I was on the edge — suicidal. I felt helpless, hopeless. Like my heart was torn in half and left incomplete. Beating, but barely. If I knew where the end of the Earth was, I'd have walked there and fallen off. There could be no greater misery. I lost the one man I still had left. I lost the man I pledged my life to — 'til death do us part. Who would've guessed that would have come so soon? Nick was so youthful, so full of life. And that life was snuffed out like a candle. Only it didn't stop burning. The pain, I mean. The deep, bullet-size hole in my heart burned in anger, in agony. The only way to cool it was with a drink — a gin and tonic, to be exact, followed by a double shot of vodka and a chaser of whiskey. And maybe a couple sleeping pills, just to ease my suffering.

Anna tried to get me to go to a counseling group for bereaved widowers. A widow at 34? How could that be? I was having trouble facing reality, she said. I admitted I was, but no amount of counseling could bring Nick back. I agreed that I would get away from the city for a few days, from all that reminded me so much of him. Anna reserved me a weekend at a resort in Connecticut whose brochure promised "a spa treatment that rejuvenates the soul and uplifts the lowest of spirits." What a crock. But I had to go—for Anna's sake.

I hadn't been totally sober since the funeral, whether it be from alcohol or the tiny white pills I took to help me sleep. Regardless, Anna thought it safer if I hired a driver, for her peace of mind she said.

I left on a Thursday morning. The driver was pleasant but didn't say much. I was glad for it. I wasn't in the mood for making idle chit-chat with a stranger. I was looking out my window as the city disappeared behind me. A refreshing breath of air filled my lungs and I suddenly felt lighter. I smiled slightly at the thought of a thousand-pound anvil— the kind Wile E. Coyote always used in a vain attempt to crush the Road Runner—with wings, flying away from me. And a piece of Grandpa Joe's advice suddenly entered my mind: "You can't carry the world upon your shoulders, Julia." No, I couldn't. And leaving the city made most of that weight vanish. But I didn't want to go to Connecticut and I didn't want to go to any damn spa. In fact, there was only one place I did want to be. It was that second that I asked the driver to take the next exit and turn around.

I was heading back to Riverdale. Where else? I realized at that moment, in the backseat of the car, that next to my daughter and Nick, whom I would never see again, Gabe was the most important person in my life. I wanted to be a part of his again. And I didn't want to just get away from the city for a weekend. I simply didn't want to live there anymore with all of its agonizing reminders. I thought about it judiciously. Nick's life insurance and investment dividends would leave Camden and me with enough to last both our lifetimes. That was no consolation, but it gave me the freedom to do what I wanted. If only I could really have what I wanted. I'd give up every last penny just to see him again. I would have been happy to live a life of poverty, if only I had Nick to live it with. I would have done anything. If I could have just one wish, I would do that day over again. His final words haunted me. *"Wish we had more time,"* he had said. If only we had known, we would have taken the time. Screw work. We would have called in sick. We would have retreated to the bedroom while Camden was still asleep and we would've made love, slowly and sweetly, like we always did. We would have spent the day together with our daughter and we would have been safe. We would have each other. But no amount of money or wishes or anything else for that matter could undo the tragedy that life had bestowed upon me.

I wasn't sure if leaving Anna was fair to Camden. They were really close and the last thing Cam needed was to lose somebody else she loved. But what else could I do? I couldn't be a good mother if I continued on the way I was. I couldn't go on there. The city had become cold and unfeeling to me. There was no escape from the memories, and as much as I didn't want to admit it, I was lonely. I needed a friend, an old friend who knew who I was before I became empty and hollow. Besides, Riverdale was a wonderful place to raise a child, I rationalized to myself.

I had been deep in thought for most of the ride. Aside from the monotonous sound of the tires rolling down the highway, it was quiet. I welcomed the silence. It gave me a chance to clear my mind and sort things out. Soon though, I drifted into a dreamy sleep. I was planting tiny purple flowers along a sidewalk that led to the front porch of a house I had never before seen. I was listening to the laughter of children whom I did not know. An old dog was lying in the grass close to me, watching me. I had flowery garden gloves on and slipped one off to pet his head. He sighed and closed his eyes for a rest. It was all so peaceful. I was content. I was happy. The sun was shining on my face. I basked in its warmth. I heard someone calling my name, a voice I did not recognize. I stood up and turned in the direction of the voice. I smiled.

Then I stirred and sat up straighter in my seat, yawning and rolling my neck to the side to get out the kink in it from sleeping for so long in the car. Before I knew it, we were pulling up in front of the Riverdale Inn. I was still tired when I got there, so I went back to sleep hoping to go back to right where I had left off.

I called Anna the next day.

"So how's the spa, girlfriend?" she asked.

"I'm not at the spa, Anna," I told her cautiously. "I'm in Riverdale."

"You're *where*?" She asked rhetorically. "Julia, what are you doing there? Why aren't you in Connecticut?"

She finally let me explain. She was understandably upset. I appreciated her pleas for me to change my mind, and trust me, if I could've convinced her to move to Ohio I would have. But Anna had been born and raised a city girl and that's where she was meant to stay, she said. For me, being in Riverdale meant being home again.

I know it may have seemed like a snap decision, but I was doing the only thing I knew to do. Move on. Isn't that what the world expects? Pick up the pieces and go on, Julia. So that's what I did. I had to.

I bought a modest house in my old neighborhood, just two blocks from where my dad's house once stood. It was hard at first. The memories would come rushing back at the strangest times. I avoided Maple Drive for quite a while. I knew I wasn't ready to drive past the empty lot.

I worked on living without Nick, as much as I hated the idea. My pain was obtrusive. It was evident even in my writing. I had been writing in a journal, to keep my sanity, but a quick glance at any given page revealed a broken heart. Like the entry I wrote the day of Nick's funeral: *The sky is cloudy, threatening a storm. The air is stagnant. Raindrops are falling from my heart. Time is standing still. Frozen. Darkness hovers over and drapes its shadows over me. The dirge is playing as wakeful sleepers walk unto the moon. Evil has prevailed. The raindrops falling from my heart are red with misery. I surrender myself to silence ~ for you, my love, have gone away.*

Some wounds would never heal. I knew that. But I had to learn to cope. At first it was a daily struggle, a juggling act between surviving and crying my eyes out. My tears once could have filled the Hudson River and now, I had no more. Sadly, I had even begun to forget the way his lips felt against mine, the way he said my name, the way he smelled. It was finally time to move on.

During his stay in New York after Nick's funeral, Gabe had gotten a nasty phone call from Cara threatening to leave him if he didn't return to Riverdale immediately. I, of course, only had knowledge of this ex post facto, or I would've intervened and insisted that he leave the city right away. He, like the Gabriel Jones I had always known, politely told Cara to shove it and I ultimately ended up being to blame. Despite the slight inconvenience of burying my husband, I was apparently a threat to Cara and her not-so-perfect relationship with Gabe. Other than the small-town rumors and salon gossip, I really didn't know much about how things were between them. What I did know was that Cara was a capricious, self-centered snob with a less-than-desirable reputation. What I didn't know was that Gabe had only been putting up with her shenanigans out of fear of losing his son, but Gabe himself spilled it all when he stopped over one night after having one too many 7 & 7s.

A persistent knock on my back door woke me shortly after I had gone to bed. When I flicked on the front porch light, I looked out to see Gabe. He winced at the brightness of the light and mumbled for me to open the door. I let him in and started a pot of coffee. We sat down on the couch and yawning, I asked him what was going on. He wasn't fall-down drunk, but he had enough to loosen his tongue.

"That bitch," he said referring to Cara, "told me that if I wanted you so bad, I could come live with you. So here I am." He laughed loud and hard. I wasn't amused.

"Gabe, seriously, how am I involved in this?" I hated being a part of their equation.

"Because I said that…" he broke off.

"You said what?" I asked, unsure if I wanted to hear the answer.

He paused for a moment and took a deep breath. "I said that I have only ever been in love with one woman and that woman is you, Julia."

Crap. I didn't know what to say. It wasn't shocking news. It was a surprise to finally hear him say it aloud, but I had always known. And deep down, it had always warmed by heart. I stared at him and he stared at me until slowly, magnetically our lips were pulled together and we kissed. It was the first time I had kissed a man since before I met Nick. I didn't feel guilty, but I worried that maybe I should have. I mean, it hadn't been *that* long. I battled my mind for a moment. *Is it too soon? Will it always be too soon? Will it ever feel right?* I was in unchartered waters. I didn't know how I should feel or what I should or shouldn't do. *You won't know, Julia, if you don't give it a shot,* my inner voice reasoned. It's kind of heartbreaking the way we go on after someone dies. I mean, if I had a choice, I would've stopped living, but I had responsibilities. I had a daughter. So what else was I supposed to do? I was human, after all, and I wasn't about to apologize to anyone for what happened next. I would not feel guilty. In fact, I downright refused to. I was taking a stand. *Yes,* inner voice, *you are right. I won't know if I am ready to move on if I am too afraid to try.* My love for Nick, I would never regret. Had he still been alive, I would have never so much as entertained the thought of leaving him for Gabe, or for anyone. Deep inside I had known for years that I loved Gabe, too, but some things just couldn't be, I thought. Our lives had gone in very different directions and we had grown apart. Still, all the signs were there—my jealousy over seeing him with Cara, the giddy way I felt when he called, the way I always longed for his comfort in times of despair. It made perfect sense. He had always been there. And better than anyone, he knew me.

I still believed with all my heart that Nick had been my soulmate, but was it possible to actually have two? Like a spare? That was the only explanation I could come up with and the only one I cared to believe. Who said I didn't deserve a second chance at happiness?

*   *   *   *   *   *   *   *   *   *   *

Perhaps it was for confirmation, perhaps for closure, but I was finally compelled to visit Nick's grave and the site where the Twin Towers once stood. Ground Zero, they called it. I made the trip to New York City alone, but I didn't keep where I was going a secret. Gabe was very supportive, agreeing that it would be good for me to go.

When I got there, I was floored at the lingering devastation that plagued the streets of lower Manhattan. Sixteen acres of unimaginable destruction. I stared, speechlessly, at the horrendous hole in the ground—the very place where so many people died, the target of an attack that caused my Nick to lose his life. It was like an open cemetery, I thought, as I watched construction workers carry loads of debris and no doubt remains out of the hole and up the ramp adorned with American flags. While I felt empathy for those who held funerals with empty caskets, I was relieved I wasn't one of them. At least I got to see Nick before he was buried. At least I had the chance to comprehend the reality of what had happened. And oh what a stark reality it had been.

As I stood there among a crowd of onlookers, I wiped away the tears as they escaped from beneath my dark sunglasses. I had lost so much there, at that very spot, and though it had once been torturous to even breathe, I suddenly felt a sense of peace and a new found clarity. At that moment, I gained a new perspective on Nick's death. He was gone, but what a way to go. What courage, what valor. Instead of being angry about him dying, I now felt pride. Yes, that's what it was. Pride. I was so very proud of him. I don't know if I would've been able to do what he did. Would I have turned around? Would I have stopped to help? Would I have risked my life or would I have just kept running? I would've liked to believe that I would have heroically endangered my own life to save another, but would I really? Would you?

At the cemetery, I knelt on the ground in front of

Nick's grave for the first time, ignoring the grass stains I was getting on my pants, and told him how sublime his departure had been. I apologized for being so furious with him. I told him that I wished to someday be half the person he had been. I told him all about Camden and how beautiful she was and how her eyes had come to look just like his, even though I was sure he already knew that. Then I told him goodbye and with my finger, I traced over the epitaph I had written for his tombstone… "The brave may not live forever, but the cautious do not live at all."

CHAPTER TWELVE

When I returned to Riverdale, I was really honestly ready to begin the next chapter in my life. I was ready to live, to laugh, to love again. Gabe said I looked as if someone had painted a rainbow over my soul. It wasn't long before he and I realized we had to chance it and throw caution to the wind. We soon fell madly in love with each other. All the suppression, the lost time, the pent-up passion exploded when we were together. We felt like sharks in a feeding frenzy. We were crazed for each other, fixated, obsessed. When he touched me, I felt alive. Even my writing had become more lighthearted. A journal entry soon after Gabe and I became involved was in sharp contrast to my earlier entries: *The clouds have vanished. I take a deep breath of fresh air. Tears of joy are flowing from my soul as time is moving on. The sun is streaming and radiates its light throughout the day. The sunset falls beyond the horizon reflecting my joy. A new day has begun. Flowers bloom into beautiful rainbows. Happiness has prevailed. Tears of joy are flowing from my soul and crying out in delectation. I surrender myself to you, for you have finally come to me.* I was actually looking toward the future instead of relentlessly dwelling on the past.

Gabe and I just couldn't get enough of each other. I craved his companionship and I know he felt the same. He said he had never been happier and I knew he hadn't. Cara was supposed to just be a temporary rebound from Gabe's jealousy over my relationship with Tom, he said. You do remember Tom, don't you? Anyway, Gabe said she never really meant that much to him. The sex was good, he admitted, but the relationship was hollow. He was planning to break it off with her until Nick called and asked him to attend the wedding.

"I couldn't show up alone," he said. "How would it have looked? Poor Gabe, giving away the girl he himself always wanted to marry. It was easier to keep up a façade," he told me late one night while we watched reruns of *All In The Family*.

When he did decide to drop Cara for good, she announced that she was pregnant. And that bond was the only thing that tied them together. And for that reason alone, Gabe continued to live with Cara while we carried on our affair. I understood his reasons and I admired his love for his son, but eventually Cara's perpetual interruptions in our life were unbearable.

"We'll fight for custody," I told Gabe confidently. "You're a great dad and Michael loves you."

"I just don't know, Jules. What if I don't get him? What then?"

He mulled over his decision for several weeks before he talked to Cara about it. As you might expect, it didn't go over very well.

"I told her I'd see her in court," Gabe told me, "And she said she'd see me in hell. She's impossible."

"So what," I said exasperated. I was fed up. I didn't want to give Gabriel an ultimatum, but I was tired of him making love to me and leaving to share a bed with Cara. I would never have him choose between his son and me—that would be downright cruel—and as a mother, I already knew who he'd pick. But something had to be done. The hold Cara had over him was ridiculous. He was clearly unhappy and we both deserved more.

"Julia," he sat beside me and looked straight into my eyes and I knew it couldn't be good.

"I love you," he said. I could hear it in his voice, the impending *but*. The ever so disconcerting *but*. Don't say it, don't say it, don't say it. I tried to will him not to.

"But I have to stay with her. For Michael's sake. Just give me a couple more months to straighten things out and I'll leave. I promise, darling."

I sighed. I sat there, still, letting it sink in.

"Okay," I said meekly. What would you have done? I wasn't willing to risk losing Gabe. I'd lost enough already. If time was what he needed, then time would be what I'd give him.

Although he never spent the night with me, he gave me all that he could and all that Cara wanted. No, I wasn't jealous of her. I was just angry that she used their little boy as a pawn in a game she'd never win. At least that's what I thought.

Several weeks after my conversation with Gabe, I woke up extremely dizzy and nauseous. *God no*, I thought, on the way to the drugstore. I couldn't believe it, but I suspected it. All that trying and timing and hoping and praying to have a baby with Nick and here I was, about to take a pregnancy test.

When I got home, I nervously tore open the wrapper and stuck the test stick between my legs. And I sat there and waited. Come on. I always have to pee. Why can't I now? *Relax*, I told myself. I was irritated and really hungry. *Come on, just pee and get this over with and then you can get some lunch*, my inner voice calmed me down. Finally. I watched anxiously as the wetness traveled up the stick and into the test window. My heart was beating fast and my head was swimming. Positive. No. It just couldn't be. But it was. Unfreakingbelievable.

After getting the official results from my doctor, I argued with myself for a few days trying to decide the best time to tell Gabe. No time seemed perfect, so I thought I might as well just get it over with. After all, this was his doing too. We met the next afternoon.

"We need to talk," Gabe announced glumly and immediately looked down sheepishly.

A Mark Twain quote quickly came to mind: *"Man is the only animal that blushes – or needs to."* Grandpa Joe had taught me long ago what it meant and I never forgot it.

"I have some news," I said trying to divert his attention to what I was about to say. But to my chagrin, he ignored me and clasped his hands together as if contemplating something very important.

I suddenly felt uneasy. Maybe he knows, I thought. Maybe he reads me so well that he already knows. Maybe he knows and he's not happy about it. It wasn't all my fault. Well, I guess it kind of was. We weren't all that careful because I thought it wasn't a possibility. Damn. I felt vomit rise up in my throat. I swallowed it down.

"I don't know how to tell you this," he began. I was fighting my nausea. "But I, uh, you should know, oh this is so damn hard." He looked up at me and I saw tears forming in the corners of his eyes.

"What? What is it, Gabe? What's wrong?" I was confused and concerned.

"Cara's pregnant," he blurted.

I said nothing. Talk about being kicked in the teeth. I couldn't fight the nausea anymore. I rushed to the bathroom and got there just in time. How could this have happened? How many times was life going to knock me down? How many times could I get back up? I steadied myself by holding onto the sides of the toilet and slowly stood up. What hurt the most was that Gabe had lied to me. He claimed he was in love with me and I truly believed he was, but he also said that he and Cara hardly spoke let alone had sex. In fact, I recalled that he told me that since he and I had gotten together, he hadn't so much as held her hand. No, I guess you didn't need to hold her hand to get her pregnant. I was hurt, distraught and furious.

"I'm so sorry, Julia," Gabe pleaded for my forgiveness.

"You don't need to apologize," I told him sternly. I don't know where the strength came from to even be able to speak. "If she is what you wanted, then what the hell were you doing with me?"

"Oh JC, *you* are who I want. I don't know how this could have happened."

"I have a pretty good idea," I muttered under my breath.

"I know it's hard to believe, but it only happened one time," he said.

"Only once, huh?" I laughed. Not a "ha ha, that's funny" laugh, but more like a "God, please help me keep my sanity" laugh.

"I swear, Julia. It was this one night—"

"Oh spare me," I interrupted him. "Like I said, you don't owe me an explanation." I think I was partially in shock. How I was keeping my cool when my hormones were raging was beyond me.

"I think I do," he said and sat down beside me at the kitchen table. I stayed there, half-listening while he carried on about some night shortly after he and I had become intimate. According to him, he didn't know what would become of us and Cara was hysterical when he told her about me. He held her while she cried and she kissed him and out of pity, he said he kissed her back and they ended up in bed. Blah, blah, blah. A sympathy fuck, more or less, he said. I rolled my eyes.

"I was thinking of you the whole time, honestly," he told me.

"So you screwed her while you thought of me" I asked crudely. "Maybe you should write for Hallmark," I said sarcastically.

"I'm ashamed of what I've done, Julia. I love you and the last thing I ever wanted to do was hurt you. I wanted to be your safety net, to protect you from ever being hurt again. But instead, I did just that. I can't tell you how very sorry I am." His puppy-dog eyes searched mine for forgiveness.

I had none. I believed that he was sorry. He seemed genuine about that, but I was in no mood for forgiving anybody. And I definitely wasn't about to tell him about our baby now. *Our baby.* Wow. What irony. A single teardrop rolled down my cheek. I felt like a wilting rose. I didn't know how many more pitfalls I could survive. Gabe reached across the table and quickly wiped my tear away with his finger. I pulled back.

"What are you going to do?" I asked him calmly, fully expecting that he'd stay with Cara but pathetically praying that he'd choose me.

"What else can I do, Julia?" he asked and that was all I needed to hear to make up my mind. Anna would get her wish after all. Camden and I were going back to New York City. Maybe my mother had it right all those years back when she left for Europe. Sometimes it's easier to run away and start anew than stay and deal with the pain. I was doing what was best for everyone, I told myself.

I didn't sell my house in Riverdale. With all that had been going on in my life, I wasn't sure I wanted to let go of my home on Birch Drive for good. I had the most beautiful tree in my backyard with a wooden bench swing under it, where I pictured myself sitting with Camden and reading her a story on a warm summer evening. And I loved my enclosed back porch. It was rustic meets shabby chic. The walls and ceiling were made of knotty pine and I had a pair of wingback chairs reupholstered in a turquoise paisley print. There was a built-in bookshelf stocked with books by my favorite authors and a small table for my laptop. It was the place I went to read, write, think. It was my sanctuary. So instead of letting it go, I rented it to a sweet young couple with false hopes of staying together forever. Honestly, they seemed in love, but what was love anyway? How bitter and cynical I had become. I didn't think I'd ever be so jaded, but life has a way of doing that.

With the house taken care of, we were on our way. Camden was thrilled to be closer to her Aunt Anna again, but I had my reservations. New York City wasn't "home" to me anymore, but staying in good ole' Riverdale was out of the question. I didn't know where I belonged. I felt like a feather, blowing in the wind, with no real place to go. I was landing here, in the city, for now. Who knew how long I'd stay. My life was filled with uncertainty. Where did I go wrong? My path had been more than difficult, yet I persevered. When would I get my reward? When would I be happy? When would I find home? Yeah, yeah— home is where the heart is, but where was mine? I'll tell you where. It had been torn apart piece by piece, time after time.

I didn't know what to do with myself, didn't know who I was anymore, didn't care. Not even Anna could console me this time. I spent most of my time at home with my daughter. Unlike my easy pregnancy with Camden, I was extremely sick. The most familiar of smells, like vanilla air freshener, would send me running to the bathroom. I had come to detest eggs and I craved peanut butter. Peanut butter crackers and peanut butter cookies, peanut butter on celery, peanut butter on pretzels, peanut butter on olives. That was my favorite. Oh, leave me be. You shouldn't knock it 'til you try it.

Anyway, I had mixed emotions about having another baby. Without a father, there wasn't anyone to share in the joy, there wasn't anyone to rub my aching feet, there wasn't anyone to argue with about baby names, there wasn't anyone to go on an olive run, there wasn't anyone to kiss goodnight. I was alone. And all the while I thought of Gabe. He should have been with me. He should be by my side. But he wasn't. He was with Cara, rubbing her feet and kissing her goodnight, I presumed.

He did miss me. I knew that. I don't know how he got my number, but he called me almost every day. I seldom answered. I didn't have anything to say. He begged for forgiveness, asked me to come back, called me stubborn, said he loved me. He even sent me a tear-jerking letter:

"My dearest Julia," it began. *"It was four months ago today that you left me. I have filled my life with work and friends, which has helped me to get through missing you so much, but even though they have filled my time, I haven't had you. With you gone, there is a piece of me missing. I want my wondrous piece back. Come back to me, Julia. I miss you terribly and I'm so incredibly sorry for hurting you. Love, Gabe."*

Part of me wanted to reach out and tell him I missed him too and that I still loved him, but the other part—the more sensible part—told me to keep my head high and ignore his apologies. Although I believed he was sorry, he was still living with Cara and I couldn't accept that. I ripped the letter to shreds and tossed it in the trash.

Anna was angry at me for concealing my pregnancy from Gabe. She said had he known about the baby, he would've been on the next plane. She said I was to blame for my situation and that if I would just stop being so foolish, I'd see that telling Gabe was in my best interest. I agreed with her that I could be obstinate at times, but I wanted Gabe to want *me* above all else, including his unborn child. I wanted Gabe to love me so much that he'd walk out on Cara, pregnant or not, and come to me. I refused to go running back to him.

After a few months, Gabe stopped calling. It was yet another blow. Even though I never spoke to him, I found comfort in hearing his voice on my machine. He'd ask how I was, how Camden was, admitted he made the biggest mistake of his life, wished that he could take it back, wished that we were kids again, wished that I would pick up the damn phone. I would listen and cry and choke on my own tears, but I wouldn't answer. I couldn't. What was there to say? He said it all when he made his decision to continue living with Cara.

I wanted to once again forget all about Gabriel Jones. I wanted to rid him from my memory, erase our past. But there was a constant reminder, a growing reminder. When the baby's due date neared, I had decided to let go of the bitter resentment I harbored toward Gabe. After all, he was the father of my baby—a baby that would someday undoubtedly want to know about their daddy. I still loved him. I didn't want to, but how could I not? I had tried to trick myself since I left Riverdale, pretending not to know any Gabriel, pretending not to long for his touch, pretending that he had been some horrible monster. But truth be told, he wasn't. He was human. The rational side of me, what little there was, knew that people were bound to make mistakes and that those same people deserve to be forgiven. Yet I couldn't. I did all I knew to do and that was to retreat. Running away had become a matter of survival.

CHAPTER THIRTEEN

The snow was beautiful. I had forgotten how beautiful New York City was in winter. It was three days before Christmas and it had been snowing all afternoon. A heavy, wet snow that blanketed the sidewalks. A pretty snow, the kind made of delicate snowflakes, each with their own exquisite design. I went out to the balcony and watched in fascination as they fell softly on my outstretched hand and quickly dissipated on my black glove. The air was frigid and I gasped as the winter wind took my breath away. Then I gasped again and again—but not for air. I was in labor.

I hurried back inside and called Anna, but there was no answer. She wasn't answering her cell phone either, so I had no choice but to call a cab. I grabbed my suitcase, which was already packed and helped Camden zip her coat, moaning louder with each sharp pang of pain.

"What's wrong, mommy?" she asked. She looked so grown up in her pink coat with her dark curls cascading from under her hood. She would soon be five years old. She was a living daily reminder of Nick. Her eyes looked just like his and she was gentle and kind like he was. She was really smart, too. She already knew how to write her name and could count to twenty-nine. She wasn't at all shy. She was assertive and strong. Her preschool teacher said she was a leader among her peers. I was so blessed with her. I loved her more than I ever thought possible.

"Is the baby hurting you?" she asked inquisitively as she scrunched up her nose. She always did that after asking a question. I found it insanely adorable, but it was all I could do to answer her without screaming at the top of my lungs. This baby would be coming much sooner than I anticipated.

Mere hours later, I was holding a baby boy in my arms. Anna had made it to the hospital just in time to coach me through the delivery. Thank God for her, I thought to myself. I was thrilled to have a son, but torn over what last name to give him. I didn't know if I should give him my last name, Stanton, or my maiden name or Gabriel's name. I had decided long ago that if I ever had a little boy, I'd name him after Grandpa Joe. It didn't seem fair to Gabe not to give him his name, but had I really been fair to Gabe for the past nine months? Suddenly, holding my baby in my arms, I regretted what I had done. He was beautiful and his dad didn't even know he existed. It wasn't too late to let him know now, was it? I was too tired to ponder it any longer. When it came time to making his name official, I just wrote it without further thought. Joseph Stanton Jones.

Camden wasn't as happy about Joey as I was.

"Why is his face all red and like squished up, mommy? He looks gross," she said and again wrinkled up her nose.

I just smiled at her childish innocence. I was overjoyed that I had a daughter and now a son as well. Even if all of my dreams hadn't come true, that one was realized. A little girl and a little boy. No, it wouldn't be perfect. How could it be when neither of them had a daddy? There was no white picket fence, but there were two beautiful amazing children—my children. And I would never let them down, I silently vowed.

I brought Joey home on Christmas Eve. What a wonderful gift he was. Camden eventually agreed that her baby brother was cute and she loved helping me with him. They were both the light of my life. I was devoted to them, day and night, and I loved them dearly, but I had begun to feel trapped, my identity lost, existing only for them. I felt guilty thinking this way. A good mother would never let such thoughts enter her mind, would she? It was selfish, I knew, but I longed for some adult company, adult conversation and sex. I wanted to work, I wanted to date, I wanted a life. My therapist agreed that I should have a life of my own, a life outside of my children. She said that if my life revolved around my children entirely, I will have nothing when they grow up and start lives of their own. I suppose she was right. I took her advice and began freelance writing when Camden went to kindergarten. Joey was nearly a year old, so I was still able to be home with him, but I was also doing something for myself and it felt good. Through my writing, I had a voice, a place for my thoughts and emotions to go.

With Anna's help, I had begun dating again. Not very often, just once or twice a month. None of them went very well, especially when I mentioned my kids. It didn't matter though. Writing was my salvation. I contemplated going back to *The Times*, but Joey had been sick lately more often than not and I didn't feel right spending time away from him.

A week after Joey's second birthday, just days before New Year's, I knew something was terribly wrong with him. He had a high fever and hadn't eaten all day. I was forcing him to drink water so he wouldn't get dehydrated. His skin was pale and I had discovered several small bruises on his legs and arms that seemed to have appeared instantly. Without hesitation, I bundled him up and headed to the emergency room. A simple blood test revealed that he was in grave danger. His white blood cell count was dangerously low. What were they saying? Some sort of cancer? Blood cancer? No, that couldn't possibly be. He was two, only two. *Oh dear God in Heaven, if you exist, you can't let this be happening.* Oh, but it was.

"Ms. Stanton," the hematologist began softly. "I have some good news and bad news."

I just stared at him. I was speechless. I knew what that opening line usually meant and I wasn't prepared to hear it. But it came anyway.

"The bad news is that Joey has what is known as A-L-L," he said. "Acute lymphoblastic leukemia."

"You, you mean cancer?" I stuttered as my stomach twisted itself into knots. I fought the vomit from rising up in my throat.

"Well yes, it is cancer. But the good news is that ALL is the most common type of childhood cancer and the most curable. When treated properly, there's a ninety-two percent chance of survival."

Despite the hopeful statistics, I was in denial.

"How could this have happened? I mean, I just took him to the doctor last week and she said Joey just had a virus. I had no reason to believe otherwise."

I felt guilty for not knowing. I was his mother and I felt like I had failed him.

"You couldn't have done anything to prevent this, Ms. Stanton," he tried to reassure me. "ALL progresses very rapidly with little or no symptoms at all. Bringing Joey to the hospital today is the best thing you could have done for him."

I placed my hand on my forehead shielding my eyes and I began to cry. But it only took a minute for mommy mode to override my self-pity.

"Now what?" I asked, ready to combat this with all that I had.

"I think we should start aggressive treatment right away," Dr. Ramero said. "We need to destroy the cancerous cells through chemotherapy. You should know, though, that it's not going to be pretty. Joey will get extremely sick until he's used to the drugs. Ms. Stanton, are you with me?"

"Uh-huh," I nodded. "Yes." I was listening, but my mind was a million miles away. I wondered if I should call Gabe.

"You'll need to sign these consent forms then," he said.

"Of course." I quickly scribbled my name on the necessary documents, giving permission for my baby to be given the chemo, without reading them. Then a phrase caught my attention. ... *bone marrow transfusion.*

"Dr. Ramero, what's this about bone marrow?"

He shook his head as if expecting my question. "In the event that Joey relapses, a bone marrow treatment may be necessary, but that's not a concern at this time." He had a nice smile.

I signed away. What else could I do? I had to put my trust into this man whom I had just met and pray that he was good at his job.

With all the formalities said and done, they finally let me see my little boy. I leaned over the bedrail and kissed his forehead. He looked up at me with big, worried eyes. "It's okay, baby. Mommy's here," I said and sang him his favorite lullaby: *"Way up yonder above the sky, a bluebird lived in a jaybird's eye ~ Buckeye Jim, you can't go, go weave and spin, you can't go ~ Buckeye Jim."*

He yawned and was fast asleep before I even finished the song, so I sat beside his hospital bed and sobbed quietly. I didn't want to wake him. I couldn't let him see how upset his mommy really was. He wouldn't understand. How could he? He was so small, so helpless, so weak. All of the tubes and monitors were scary enough for him. It only took a day for him to learn that nurses meant pain. He cried every time one came near him, fearing they would be sticking him with yet another needle. I read a pamphlet about implanted catheters and campaigned for him to get what they called a Hickman. I had never heard of it, but from what I understood, all of Joey's pain meds and IV fluids would go in through one tube and he wouldn't have to endure any more needles. The nurses could even draw his blood samples from it.

Dr. Ramero said he'd see to it right away if I was sure I wanted it. I asked him why he didn't tell me about it. He explained that it required two small incisions in the upper chest and had to be inserted into one of the main veins near the heart. He said it had its own set of complications and had extensive care instructions. I told him I'd think about it some more.

Camden had been staying with Anna since I was spending most of my time at the hospital. I left only to shower and change my clothes. I tried to spend some time with Camden, but her endless stream of questions were tiring.

"Is Joey going to die, mommy?", "Can I get his disease if I sleep with his teddy bear?", "When is he coming home?"

LAURA LEIGH LESKOVAC

I know it sounds terrible, but it was actually a relief to go back to the hospital. Anna picked up the
pieces for me, as usual, but she had been nagging at
me about calling Gabe and I was getting extremely
annoyed with her. I know I was overly emotional and
somewhat irrational, but I had a right to be for God's
sake. So I told her to just lay off and give me a fucking
break. As if I didn't contemplate it every day. But bottom line, it was none of her damn business.

Joey was getting worse by the day. Dr. Ramero
said he'd be sick, but I didn't expect to see him struggling as much as he was. Then came the final blow. It
was mid-afternoon on a Tuesday when the doctor sat
down with me and said Joey wasn't responding to the
chemo the way he had hoped.

"I'm afraid we have no other choice," he said to
me solemnly.

He would need a bone marrow transplant and
without it, he wouldn't live longer than a year. His
little life flashed before my eyes. My poor baby. He
didn't deserve to be going through this. It was me
who should have been punished. I was his mother. It
should have been me. And all the while, in the back of
my mind, was the fact that I had deprived him of a
father. However short his life would be, it was thus far
without a daddy and there was nobody to blame for
that except me. Me and my damn stubbornness. Me
and my foolish pride.

The transplant wasn't an option—it was a matter
of life or death. Dr. Ramero placed Joey on the waiting
list, but he warned me that the list was longer than the
time we had."The most probable matches come from

blood relatives, especially siblings that share the same parents," he said. "His sister would be his best shot."

But I knew she wouldn't. Dr. Ramero didn't know that Joey and Camden didn't have the same father.

"Camden is his half-sister," I said quietly. Not out of shame, but out of guilt. I couldn't escape from the thought of Gabe and how I had wronged both him and *our* son.

"Oh," he replied quickly and looked down at his shoes. "Then we may have a problem."

Dr. Ramero said it was a longshot, but still worth a try, so Camden was tested anyway. She was a brave little girl and didn't make a peep as the kind nurse drew her blood. She beamed when the nurse told her what a big girl she was and gave her a princess sticker. But as suspected, she wasn't a match.

I was next. I prayed at least a hundred times that I would be a match. It was the only way I could help him. Maybe this would be my chance. Maybe this could right the wrong that I had done. I could be a match. I was his mother, after all. But no such luck. I felt awful. I couldn't protect him. I couldn't help him. I had let him down once again.

I took a deep breath. I knew what I had to do.

CHAPTER FOURTEEN

So I took a deep breath, I swallowed my pride and I dialed his number. I didn't have a choice. My baby depended on me. His life depended on Gabe. I held my breath while I waited for him to answer. My heart was beating extremely fast and the lump in my throat was enormous. What nerve I had calling him after nearly three years had gone by. Six rings, seven, eight. *Oh, please pick up. I don't know if I'll have the guts to call again.* Nine, ten.

"Hello?" he answered annoyed and breathless.

I didn't know where to begin. I had rehearsed the call for the past hour in my head, but my mind was suddenly blank.

"Hello?" he asked again.

"Hi," was all I could say. "It's me."

"My God, Julia, is it really you?" he asked incredulously.

"Yes, Gabriel, it's me."

"How are you? Is everything okay?" He was the same old Gabe—concerned and caring even after all the time that had passed.

"No, Gabe. Everything's not okay," I answered truthfully.

"What is it? Is there anything I can do?"

"Actually, there may be," I said cautiously.

"Jules, are you in trouble?"

I was overcome with emotion—part of me loving that he seemed to still care about me, part of me hating him for not caring enough to fight for me. I started sobbing so hard that I couldn't answer him.

"JC, talk to me. What's going on?"

"Oh, Gabe," I said between choked tears. "I, I, I need your help." I couldn't just tell him over the phone.

"I'll be there. Just tell me where."

His response threw me off guard. It was what I had wanted to hear him say, but I couldn't believe he did. Was his love for me unconditional? Was it me who didn't fight for him? *I told you he still loved you,* my inner voice taunted.

I asked him to come to the New York Downtown Hospital. I didn't say why. He didn't ask. I told him that Anna would meet him in the main lobby.

"It's at 170 William Street. Be safe on your way," I told him before I hung up.

The hours seemed like days while awaiting Gabe's arrival. I paced the hallway outside of Joey's room, biting my fingernails, trying to imagine Gabe's reaction when I introduced him to his son for the first time. I now knew that I had done both of them a grave injustice. Who was I to decide that Gabriel shouldn't be a part of Joey's life? I had stupidly let my stubbornness blind my judgment. *Yes, inner voice, you were right. I selfishly made decisions that affected lives other than my own.* I hated myself at that moment. What had I done? I wasn't any better of a person than my mother had been. I was just like her. I shuddered at the realization. Could Gabriel ever forgive me? I was hugging myself with my own arms. The tears streamed down my face and I leaned back against the green tile wall before I slid down onto the cold, dirty floor and held onto my knees, rocking back and forth. *Oh, Grandpa, I could really use your shoulder to lean on,* I thought to myself.

A nurse walked by slowly before stopping and stooping down to see if I was okay. I wiped my nose and cheek with the backside of my hand, and sniffling, I said I was alright. I had to pull it together. Gabe would be arriving soon and I would surely need my strength for that. I had no idea how he would take my sudden confession. He was a loyal, understanding man, but he would have every right to be angry when he found out about Joey. Did I say angry? More like extremely pissed off.

I glanced at my watch and was surprised at how late it was. I had my wits about me enough to care about how I looked though. I knew I had cried off my makeup and probably had black smudges under my eyes, so I retreated to the bathroom and cleaned myself up.

Even though I hated the reason for Gabe coming to New York, it would be the first time I saw him in years. I stared at myself in the mirror. I looked tired and old. My eyes were bloodshot.

Since Joey was born, I had imagined what I would say to Gabe should we ever see each other again, but when it counted, the words had escaped my memory. I had no clue where I was going to begin. Should I greet him with a nonchalant, "Hey Gabe, this is your son." No, that was too shocking. How about, "Guess what? I had a baby. He's yours." No, too insensitive. What in the hell was I going to say? I supposed I could try the truth for a change.

Anna was waiting for Gabe in the lobby so that I could stay by Joey's side. He was tired and he wanted me to sing to him.

"Mommy's here, baby," I comforted him. And I sang softly, as was our nightly ritual. *"Way up yonder above the moon, a blue jay nest in a silver spoon ~ Buckeye Jim, you can't go, go weave and spin, you can't go ~ Buckeye Jim."*

He fell fast asleep and I kissed his forehead. "Daddy will be here soon," I told him, knowing he couldn't hear me, but saying it out loud to make it seem more real. I decided to switch Anna places. I wanted to talk to Gabriel first before Anna had to dodge too many questions. She wished me luck and said she'd be waiting in Joey's room. I told her that Gabe and I would probably leave the hospital briefly so we could talk privately. She said she'd call my cell phone if there were any critical changes. My little boy had been comfortably stable for the past couple days, but nothing remained constant. He had been in the pediatric unit for longer than ten weeks already. The hospital had become my home. I welcomed the idea of getting away for a while.

I sat in one of several plastic-covered chairs in the lobby, leafed through a magazine and put it back down. Who was I kidding? I couldn't concentrate on anything. I stared out the window deep in thought. It had begun snowing and I hoped that Gabe had a safe flight. Any minute now. I anxiously glanced at the automatic sliding doors every two or three seconds. My throat was dry and my bottom lip was numb from chewing on it. How complicated life had been since our days at Riverdale High. I wondered if Gabe had changed at all or if he still looked like the handsome, rugged Gabe I had always known. I didn't have to wonder for long. The doors slid open like they had done forty times before, but this time, he walked in. He was obviously unsure of what to expect as he nervously glanced around the room. He looked right past me and headed toward the information window.

"Gabriel!" I called. And he turned around, set down his suitcase and stared at me.

I walked toward him cautiously. He looked good, as usual, wearing his Levi's and a mock turtleneck olive green sweater under his black leather jacket.

"Julia!" He opened his arms wide to hug me. I immediately responded by slipping my arms around his back and rested my head against his chest. He felt so good. So familiar. It had been a long time since I'd been hugged by a man. Three years ago, to be exact, when I left Gabe. For so long I had been greeted by empty arms and I had become empty inside. Tears formed in the corners of my eyes and I stepped back and looked into his eyes.

"Why did you leave me, Jules? Why didn't you return any of my calls?" He asked and I felt as if I had been slapped across the face. I certainly wasn't expecting that barrage right away. As if he even had any right to ask me that after what he had done. I didn't say a word and I think he read the concern on my face.

"We'll talk about it later," he said. "But tell me, what's going on? I've been a nervous wreck since I got your call. You look good. Are you sick?"

"Maybe we should go somewhere and sit down," I suggested. "There's a quiet place on the corner that serves great tea."

The five-minute walk to Ginny's Teapot was the most uncomfortable silence I had ever experienced. It was still snowing and I turned up the collar on my coat. I was arguing with myself over what to ask him about first. Should I ask about his kids? No, his kids were also Cara's and I felt nothing but resentment toward her. Should I ask him about Riverdale? No, that would just make me homesick. Should I ask about his job? No, that's the first thing you ask an old college roommate, not someone you were madly in love with. What to say, what to say. Then he spoke. Thank God.

"Julia, is something wrong with Camden?" I knew he was wondering why the hell I had called him after all this time and asked him to come to a hospital. "I sure have missed that little girl."

"No, Camden's fine. She's full of too many questions, but she's fine."

"A chatterbox like her mom, I suppose," he said and smiled.

I had become a regular at Ginny's since Joey had first gone into the hospital and Sunday nights were never busy, so I knew we'd be able to carry on a private conversation with little interruption. I sat down in the booth farthest to the back and Gabe slid in across from me. The tea shop was decorated with Victorian-style paintings and on each table were fancy little lamps with lacy shades that cast a golden glow. It was a comforting atmosphere, which is why it had become my sanctuary when I needed a little time away from the hospital.

We ordered drinks and I knew my stalling was over. It was time.

"First, I really appreciate that you came here, Gabe. You have no idea how much it means to me," I said.

"I'm happy that you called," he said. "I'm just not sure yet of the circumstances."

"Gabriel," I began slowly. I was fighting back the tears already. "I need to start at the beginning and then you'll know why I've asked you to come to the city."

"I'm listening," he said as he opened a packet of sugar.

And sitting there at Ginny's Teapot, I told him why I left. I told him about the pregnancy. I told him that I hadn't wanted to compete with Cara for his love. I told him it was the hardest decision I ever had to make and I told him that I now realized how selfish that decision was. He didn't say much. I talked and he listened. I only had a couple sips from my tea, but Gabe had three cups already. Out of nervousness, I think. His face remained expressionless for the most part and he didn't say a word to me. But I knew Gabe well enough to know that his silence was much worse than anything he could have possibly spoken. I got as far as giving birth to a son and paused to add some hot water to my tea.

"And the baby, Julia? What happened to your, er, our baby?" he asked.

"He's in the hospital, Gabriel." I was so nauseous. "That's why I called you. He has leukemia."

"What?" he snapped. "How long have you known?" He ran his fingers through his hair, trying to keep his cool but I could tell he was angry.

"Since the end of December."

"So why now? Why are you telling me this now? You suddenly care?" He was clearly upset and had every right to be. *He's going to leave. He's going to tell you he doesn't ever want to see you again.* Wow. *You really messed this up.* I wished my inner voice would just hush. But she was right. *Please don't go*, I silently pleaded. *Please don't walk out of here and leave me. I know I deserve it, but please, please, I love you and I need you.* But I kept my thought to myself. Too much, too soon.

Instead, I told him about the bone marrow transplant and that neither Camden nor I were matches.

"You may be the only possible living match, Gabe," I said dismally.

"What do you mean by *living match*?" he asked.

"Dr. Ramero, Joey's doctor, said that siblings are the most probable matches and he mentioned that many couples even have another baby hoping the newborn is an exact bone marrow match for their other child," I explained.

"Julia, are you asking me to get you pregnant?"

I was so surprised that I laughed loudly, really loud. For the first time in two months, I laughed.

"Oh no. No, no, no, no, no, no. The thought never entered my mind," I lied. Of course I had thought about it once or twice before, but I dismissed it as a ridiculous unrealistic notion.

"I don't think Cara would go for that anyway," I said.

"Julia, I'm not going to pretend that I'm not upset about you keeping my son a secret from me. And then I find out about him only after he's become ill. I can't believe you would do this to me."

I stared into my empty mug. I was so ashamed. I couldn't believe I had done this to him either. But still, a part of me felt it was his fault too. If he was committed to me, he never should have had sex with Cara. The thought still disgusted me.

"This is just a lot to grasp right now," he continued. "But it's time I'm straight with you, too."

I sat across from Gabe—Gabriel Jones, my childhood friend, my ex-lover, my baby's father—and listened intently as he had just listened to me.

What he said surprised me nearly as much as I had surprised him. A month after Cara gave birth to a baby girl, they were having a heated argument when Cara blurted that Gabe wasn't the baby girl's father. Gabe said he had become accustomed to her malicious comments, so he brushed it off as he normally did. But later that week, he overheard Cara on the phone and became suspicious that she was seeing somebody else on the side. When he confronted her about it, she denied it vehemently. He said he believed her at the time.

"How stupid I was," he said. "I believed every one of her fucking lies."

I started to say something. I wanted to tell him that believing somebody, trusting somebody, wasn't a fault—it was only human. I had learned my lesson from Tom, I mean Preston, whoever the hell he was, and I knew all too well how stupid someone can make you feel. But Gabe held up his hand in protest, interrupting me.

"Just let me continue, please. I haven't talked to anybody about this until now and it's harder than I thought it would be," he said.

I shook my head in understanding and he went on. Apparently Cara had been seeing someone else or sleeping with someone else. Gabe questioned the dates of his daughter's conception and painfully insisted upon a paternity test. He was understandably torn. He said he couldn't bear the thought of losing his little girl, but he'd rather find out sooner than later. With tears in his eyes, he filled me in on all the despicable details. What a deceitful bitch Cara had been.

Turns out, the baby wasn't his. Even more heartbreaking was that Michael wasn't his biological son either. I was in tears by this point as well and I reached across the table and grasped Gabe's hands in mine. What kind of woman would hurt my Gabe this way? A monster, that's who. I was furious.

My eyes blazed with ire as Gabe finished his horror story of betrayal. As hard as it was for him, he forced Cara to leave his house and he began distancing himself from her children. He took her to court in hopes of gaining joint custody of his son on the grounds that he had been the only father Michael had ever known, but he lost.

"The part of my heart that I still had after you left was ripped out when I lost my kids," he said. "Poof. Just like that."

Nothing that I could say would erase his misery, except maybe one thing.

"I still love you, Gabriel," I said sheepishly. "I never stopped."

He gripped my hands tighter as I continued.

"I know it's no consolation, but you do have a son. There are no words for how deeply I regret my decisions. I don't expect you to forgive me, at least not right away. I robbed you of your right as a father and worst of all, I have robbed us of two precious years out of our lives," I choked on my own tears. "Two years that could have been wonderful and fulfilling. I can never forgive myself for losing that time. But right now, your little boy needs you. And he is *your* little boy, Gabe."

Gabe stood up hastily and I feared that he was going to dismiss all that I had just told him and that he'd walk right out of Ginny's Teapot without turning back. *Please God, no. Please don't let him go. Please, please, please. Please tell me you're sorry again and let me accept your apology this time. Please tell me you forgive me. Please tell me you still love me. Please say you'll help Joey. Please, please.*

He extended his hand toward me to help me up from my seat and we stood, face to face, and stared at each other for a moment. My eyes searched his, trying to read his thoughts, but I had absolutely no idea what he was thinking.

"I forgive you," he said and kissed me on the forehead. Wow. Although I was hoping and praying for it, that was the last thing I expected to hear.

"And I never stopped loving you either, JC." I think my heart stopped for a second. "Now I believe there's a little guy who is waiting for his daddy and he's been waiting long enough."

CHAPTER FIFTEEN

Back at the hospital, I peered into Joey's room before Gabe and I entered. I didn't want to wake him if he was still sleeping, but he wasn't. He was wide awake and asking Anna where his mommy was.

I walked in gingerly, unsure of his reaction to Gabe. Anna stood up right away, smiled at Gabe and excused herself from the room. Visiting hours were almost over, but there was enough time to introduce Gabe to his son.

"Mommy!" Joey yelled, happy to see me.

"Hi love bug," I leaned over his bed and kissed him.

He looked up at Gabe suspiciously. "Doc-tah?" he asked.

Gabe looked at me to interpret.

"He thinks you're a doctor," I said amused.

"No buddy," Gabe laughed. "I'm not a doctor."

"Joey, this is the man mommy told you about," I said. There was no easier way to tell him, no easier way to help him understand. So I drew in a deep breath and just said it. "He's your daddy."

Wide-eyed and curious, Joey studied Gabe for a moment and must have decided he was family already. "Me toy?" he asked.

"Oh Joey," I moaned. I turned to Gabe. "He wants to know if you brought him a toy," I explained. "Sorry."

"It's okay," Gabe said to me and turned back to our son. "I do have a surprise for you, but it will have to wait until tomorrow. So you better get some rest, buddy and I'll see you in the morning."

He kissed Joey goodnight and told him they'd have plenty of time to get to know each other. Despite his pleas to have his surprise right then, it didn't take long for him to settle down and fall asleep. Though I usually slept on a fold-out cot in his room, I left that night with Gabriel and went back to my apartment.

I wasn't at all prepared for what happened next, but I didn't fight it either. I was in the midst of insisting that Gabe take my bed and I would sleep on the sofa, when he shushed me by placing his finger over my lips. When I didn't shut up, he covered his mouth over mine to cease my further protest.

And what a kiss it was. I didn't resist. I didn't want to, so why should I? Gabe and I had bad timing, that was for sure, but we still loved each other. And besides, I was a grown woman with womanly needs. I kissed him back harder than he kissed me. He must've taken my reaction as a green light. In seconds, his hands were traveling all over my body. Up my shirt squeezing my breasts, down my pants rubbing my backside. He unbuttoned my blouse with a ravenous desire and flicked my nipples with his tongue, awakening a carnal desire inside of me that had been dormant for years.

Gently, he pushed me onto the bed where he pinned me down and circled my lips with his tongue and slowly moved downward, kissing every inch of my body and stopping to pay special attention to my breasts once again. When he reached my waist, he hastily pulled down my pants and jammed a finger deep inside of me. And then another. His touch was dangerously refreshing. He soon replaced his finger with his tongue and drove me absolutely crazy. I twisted around, squirming with pleasure. I reached for him. Mmm, he was hard. Really hard. My heart raced with anticipation. I craved him. I wanted him inside of me so badly. It seemed like forever while I waited for him to fill me up, but it was worth the wait. I screamed out in ecstasy. His appetite for my body was insatiable. We fucked for hours that night, orgasm after orgasm, breaking only to catch our breaths and reposition ourselves until we eventually collapsed, naked and weary.

When I woke up the next morning, I was surprised to see him actually lying next to me. It wasn't a dream after all. Gabriel Jones was in my bed—lying nude and irresistible. I lay beside him, twirling his dark brown chest hair, until he awakened.

"Good morning, Jules," he said as he struggled to open his eyes.

"Morning, sleepyhead." I couldn't stop smiling.

"What time is it?" he asked.

"Time to get up!" I teased and pulled his pillow from under his head. We laughed and fooled around a bit more before actually getting out of bed.

"I really did miss you, JC," Gabe said as we headed out the door that afternoon.

It was strange the way we picked up right where we left off—in our relationship, I mean. He was so forgiving, it almost made me sick. I wasn't willing or able to forgive him that easily, so I didn't really think I deserved the same in return. It made me love him even more. When I left Riverdale, I had no idea Gabe and I would be together again. Sadly, it sometimes takes a tragedy or in my case a desperate call for help, for people to realize their true feelings, but I never expected it to start like it had. If there was anything positive to come from Joey's illness, it was finding each other again. Of course I'd rather have lived a lifetime of misery and loneliness than to have my little boy fighting to survive, but now that Gabe and I were together, I planned to make damn sure I never lost him again.

*   *   *   *   *   *   *   *   *   *   *

It was Monday morning—the start of a new week and hopefully a new life. After getting showered and dressed, we went to the hospital. After the initial promising blood test results came back, Dr. Ramero put Gabe on the donor priority list and he was scheduled for the donation procedure the next day.

It was 7 a.m. when they took Gabe into the operating room. The entire process took less than an hour. Gabe was prepped for the procedure and given general anesthesia. Dr. Ramero explained that they would withdraw the bone marrow from Gabe's hipbone by inserting a large needle into it several times—up to fifty times, he said. I winced at the thought, but I wouldn't have hesitated if I had been a match. When it came to fighting Joey's illness, I felt helpless. All I had was faith and all I could give was my love, but I had come to know that sometimes love just isn't enough. Everything depended on this. *Please, please let this work. It just has to. Don't let my baby die. He's so little, so innocent, so young.*

Gabe's marrow was a partial match, but partial was better than nothing. My fingers were crossed in hopes that Joey's little body wouldn't reject it. I couldn't wait for him to get Gabe's marrow, but before the actual transplant, his own bone marrow had to be destroyed so that the remaining cancer cells would be eradicated, making room for the new marrow. To do that, he would be given chemotherapy for four straight days. The transplant would finally be two days after that, giving him one day to rest and recuperate.

Gabe and I never left his side. We watched as the bone marrow was transfused into our son. It was just like a blood transfusion. Dr. Ramero told us it would be two to six weeks for the new marrow to begin producing healthy blood cells and platelets. Joey responded to the transplant with only a few minor complications. He was a fighter, our little guy.

It took nearly a year for Joey's counts to go back to normal and for our lives to finally become somewhat normal again. During that time, Gabe had traveled back and forth between Riverdale and New York on weekends. He had begged me to come back to Ohio with him every time he left, but I didn't want to switch Joey's doctors. They had become like a second family to him.

Gabe and I had been carrying on like newlyweds since we reunited the previous winter. With Joey's cancer in remission, we actually had a chance to think about the future. I had gotten over asking myself if I deserved another chance at happiness. Of course I did. All I had ever done is loved—loved unconditionally, loved too much. And I had learned that for as much joy love brings, there's even more pain when it's gone. Like Simon & Garfunkel said: *"If I'd never loved, I never would have cried."* But even in hindsight, I still would have loved. And loved, and loved. The pain wouldn't stop me from loving again—it couldn't. I had too much to give.

When it came to love, I was a fighter. My scars—my emotional scars—only served to remind me of that fight. My favorite lines from "The Boxer" came back to me: *"In the clearing stands a boxer, and a fighter by his trade ~ And he carries the reminders of every glove that laid him down or cut him, 'til he cried out in his anger and his shame, I am leaving, I am leaving, but the fighter still remains..."*

I would always fight for love, I knew that, but I wished I wouldn't always have to. Though I was confident that Gabe loved me more than ever, I had caught myself staring at my naked left hand a lot. I had taken off my ring from Nicholas on the day of his funeral and put it away for Camden to one day have. If someone had told me beforehand that my fairytale wouldn't last long, I would have ignored their warnings and lived it anyway. It was hard to believe he'd been gone so long already.

Gabe and I hadn't discussed marriage, at least not seriously, but I didn't have a doubt that would be the next step for us to take. I thought about it often. I imagined where we would be if and when he finally asked. Then, after some considerable time had passed, he seemed oblivious to the idea, but I still thought about it constantly, always wondering why he hadn't yet asked, always wondering what he was waiting for. I knew that I knew that I knew that he didn't want to be with anyone else and that he was perfectly content with our relationship. But his avoidance of the subject proved that he didn't care about my discontentment.

I dared to ask him about it late one night after the kids had gone to bed.

"I don't understand what you're so upset about," was his reply to my inquisition.

"Of course you don't," I said snidely and left the bedroom. I was not going to sleep in the same bed with a man who didn't understand how I felt nor was willing to see my perspective. I was preparing the sofa for myself when he emerged from the bedroom wearing only his Calvin Klein boxers.

"Why are you doing this?" he asked, scratching his head.

I ignored him.

"Why are you sleeping out here alone?" he asked again. And for the second time, I didn't answer. How couldn't he get it? He was an intelligent man, yet he was clueless.

He turned around and went back to the bedroom. When I heard the door close, I had to bite my tongue to stop myself from screaming at him, for fear that I'd wake the children. What a jerk, I thought.

I lay there fuming, wondering how he could just walk away and go to sleep while I was so distraught over his procrastination. Of course, one can only procrastinate on something they intend to eventually do and I knew not of his intentions. Like I said, I knew he loved me, but love wasn't everything and whoever said it was must have been wearing rose-colored glasses.

And I knew I sounded insecure when I harassed him for answers, but what else could I do? I was feeling foolish. Waiting for him to ask me to become his wife had begun to consume me. What was keeping him from proposing? I mean, we had a great relationship. Our sex life was incredible. We had made every indication to one another that we planned to be in this for the long haul. Every indication that is, except a ring.

He could tell me he loved me until the end of time and still, it wouldn't be enough without that ring—without making it official—without claiming me as his own for once and for all—without shouting to the world that I was the one he wanted to spend eternity with—without that damn diamond.

Don't get me wrong. It wasn't the ring I was obsessed about. I didn't want a fancy one, didn't want a monstrous rock. Simple was better. Just a circle of gold—a circle that signified a never-ending romance, a circle that signified a unified bond that refused to be broken.

Forgive me for whining, but I wanted to wear the glass slipper. I needed him to prove how deep his love for me ran. I needed results—not excuses. And I was beginning to resent him for making me beg. Sometimes I felt like he even reveled in my groveling. Ring anxiety, Anna called it. But really, it was much more than that.

After Nick died I thought I'd never get married again, but Gabe happened. It took me a long time to accept that I would be somebody else's wife and would once again want to claim somebody else's name. No longer Julia Clydesdale Baker. No longer Julia Clydesdale Stanton. Instead, Julia Clydesdale Jones. It would take getting used to, but I was ready. Gabriel apparently was not.

As usual, Anna didn't keep her thoughts to herself.

"I don't know what I'd do," she said to me one afternoon over the phone. "But I do think it's ridiculous. I mean, what's he so afraid of? If you ask me, I'd say why pay for the milk when he's getting the cow for free?"

I could always count on Anna for her sensitivity. But she did make a point. I no doubt was in love with Gabriel, but again, what was keeping him from going all in and vowing to love me forever? All I had done my whole life was love, and all I ever wanted was to be loved... and for once, I didn't want that love to be temporary. I seemed to endlessly be in transition and I was ready for something more permanent, more concrete. Something immortal.

I asked Anna if she thought moving closer to him would help give him the push he needed. Maybe closing the distance gap would be good for us. She listened as I basically answered my own questions and then agreed with whatever I was saying. I once read somewhere that when you seek advice, you're actually looking for an accomplice. When I asked Anna what to do about Gabe, I knew that she'd agree with me, but I needed to hear it—to hear that somebody else was on my side, to hear that somebody else still believed in love.

I had decided to leave New York City for once and for all. If I should ever up and run again, I wouldn't be heading there. Anna and Dolen were moving to the suburbs and other than Ross, Ed Garrison and a few social acquaintances, I had nobody in the city who really mattered to me. Again, I would drift from one place to another, if need be, before I washed up somewhere that I could call home. For now I was going back to the one place I could still call home and that was Riverdale. Riverdale—with all of its quirks and all of its familiarities. Riverdale—with all of the qualities that makes a hometown "home."

I moved back into my vacant house on Birch Drive. The couple that was renting it didn't renew their lease, so there she sat, waiting for my return. Like a vessel, empty and vast, quietly tarrying, sitting still as long as necessary—ready to be filled with warmth and laughter and the pitter patter of playing children and maybe even the heavy trod of a cavorting dog. A dog that didn't yet exist, that wasn't yet a part of our family. A dog that, despite Camden's pleas, I hadn't yet given in to and agreed to get. But maybe I was softening.

CHAPTER SIXTEEN

We named him Blackjack. Our new puppy, that is. He was the most adorable little black pup, despite his big disproportional ears that he hadn't yet grown into. His eyes were droopy and he had a short, stubby tail that wagged ceaselessly. He hadn't yet learned to effectively bark. Rather, it was a tiny squeak that seemed to even take him by surprise when it eeked out.

I accepted an editing position at *The Riverdale Press*—the very place I had strived to get away from years before. It's funny how life can end up becoming one colossal circle, ending where you started. My first day back was unsurprisingly uneventful. The upcoming mayoral election was the only news worth reporting. And really, it wouldn't have been that interesting at all except that the mayor's seat was being challenged by his ex-wife and the mudslinging campaign was already in full force. I had to remind myself that sleepy Riverdale was the polar opposite of New York City, but it would take some getting used to again and it wasn't easy to stay hopeful when everything seemed so dim. I was depressed and trying to resist the urge to drink, but I was too weak. I wanted nothing more than to wallow in my own self-pity.

On my way home, I stopped at Pete's, an old-fashioned bar with a rinky-dink dance floor and a poor selection of booze, but it would do. A scotch on the rocks, please. That had been Nick's usual. I drank it for him, in his honor. Then a gin & tonic. That's what Tom always drank. Here's to you Tom, or whoever you are, wherever you are, you rotten fink. And a Miller Lite for good 'ole Gabe. Better stick to beer now, I thought to myself, remembering my grandpa's drinking wisdom. *"Liquor before beer, you're in the clear."* But I wasn't in the clear. Far from it. My senses were becoming dull. Dull and unfeeling, yet so sentimental. Too damn sentimental.

I sat there, silently drinking my bottle of beer and taking in all that was happening around me. I felt like the center of a carousel. The part that doesn't go up, just goes around and around. The part that nobody ever pays attention to. A wallflower I had never been, but there at that moment, I faded into the background easily and effortlessly. Life was circling around me and there I was. Sitting, watching. Not participating, not wanting to.

I watched a good-looking man in khakis and an orange polo shirt slip onto the empty barstool next to a pretty twenty-something dark-haired girl and was reminded of when Tom swept me off my feet at Rick's Café. I slowly turned my head and was entranced by a couple sitting across from each other in a booth. They were sharing a basket of fries and acting as if they were the only two people in the world. I watched her while she flaunted her left hand at him, purposefully catching her diamond in the light. He smiled back at her, reached across the table and kissed her hand ever so gently. They looked so in love, so innocent, so naïve. I couldn't get over how much he resembled Nick, right down to his crooked smile.

I closed my eyes in remembrance. When I opened them, I gazed at a woman sitting across from me, alone, also drinking a Miller Lite. I tipped my beer to her and she did the same. She looked so lonely, so forlorn. I smiled at her and she smiled in return, but she wasn't happy. That much was obvious. She had a few tiny wrinkles at the corners of her eyes and she looked a bit aged beyond her time. Maybe from being hurt so much. Maybe from dealing with a lifetime of sadness. Maybe from not having a mother to tell her that it's never too early to moisturize.

I stared at her, studying her, but she didn't seem to mind. Her hair was the same color as mine and her eyes looked vaguely familiar. A tall brown-haired man with deep-set eyes sat down next to her and said something to her, but she didn't answer. She didn't even acknowledge his presence. She just sat there, staring at me.

"Julia," I thought I heard someone say.

"Julia. Is the mirror really that fascinating?" he asked.

I turned in his direction and then quickly back to the woman across from me. The man sitting beside her looked just like Gabe.

"Julia, look at me," he said and I turned again and faced him. "I thought I might find you here. What are you doing?"

"What does it look like?" I snapped at him.

"It looks like your running away again," he said.

"So what if I am? Maybe that's all I know to do. And who really gives a shit."

"I do," Gabe said firmly. "I love you, dammit."

"Love, shmuv. What a crock. Who needs it anyway?" I was drunk. No denying that. But I was onto something. What did love ever do for me? I had fallen in love three times and three times I had been crushed, robbed of my happiness and falsely tricked into believing that I couldn't live without it. I was such a fool. Deceived by life again and again. I had played all my cards and was left with nothing. No ace up my sleeve this time.

"Julia, you're drunk and I'm taking you home," he said sternly.

"Home. Now there's an illusion. Where *is* home, Gabriel? Tell me, please. I'd love to know."

Gabe couldn't answer me. Instead, he ignored me, took me back to my house and helped me inside. I was uncooperative to say the least and fought him tooth & nail while he struggled to take off my shoes and jeans. I don't remember what happened after that, but I woke up the next morning with an incredible hangover and Gabriel lying next to me.

It took a few moments to realize what I had done the night before.

"My God! The kids!" I yelled.

Gabe stirred and sat up in bed amused as I hurriedly threw on some pants.

"Julia, the kids are fine. They're still sleeping," he said. "The babysitter called me when you didn't come home."

I rubbed my temples, trying to collect my thoughts. My head was aching. No, it was pounding. Oh what a headache. I managed to utter a "thank you" and headed to the bathroom for a cold shower. I emerged with a towel wrapped around my body and another around my hair. Gabe was awake, but still lying in bed with his arms crossed behind his head.

I rummaged through my drawer for a pair of underwear and a bra. I could feel him watching me, but I pretended not to notice. I slipped on my panties under my towel and spritzed on some body spray.

"Thanks for taking care of the children," I said without turning around. "You can go now."

"What? You're kicking me out?" he asked laughing.

"I'm serious, Gabe. I want you to leave."

He sauntered toward me and bent down to kiss my neck. I turned around abruptly.

"Gabe, stop."

"You know you want it," he teased.

"Yeah, well I want a lot of things."

"Not that again," he moaned.

"Yes, *that* again," I sighed.

"Julia, you are the love of my life, the mother of my child. Isn't that enough?"

"No," I replied sharply. He was becoming intolerable.

"I was thinking...maybe we should move in together," he said. "We never really lived together. Full time, I mean."

"Oh, I see. I'm good enough to live with but not to marry."

"That's not what I said," he said defensively.

"You didn't have to."

"Jules, please. Why is this so important to you?"

"Why *isn't* it important to you?" I shot back. I was becoming angrier by the second.

"Of course it is...someday," he answered slowly.

"What is it you're waiting for?" I asked in a pissy tone. "It's not like we're getting any younger."

"I'm just not ready, I guess," he finally admitted.

"That's just great, Gabriel. When you figure out what you want, call me. Until then, don't bother." I picked up his shirt and heaved it at him before I stormed out of the room. I was at a point in my life where I didn't want to play any more games and I didn't have room for anyone else who was too scared to get their feet wet. Either jump in or step down. There was no in-between. For once, I was calling the shots. And it felt good to be in control.

Life had thrown one too many curveballs and now it was my turn to stand on the pitcher's mound.

*   *   *   *   *   *   *   *   *   *

I ordered pizza for dinner and Camden had persuaded Joey to watch *Little Mermaid* for the hundredth time, so while I poured drinks, they started the movie. It was seven o'clock. That's when the phone rang. I answered it quickly, hoping that Gabe had come to his senses after all.

"Hel-lo," I said in a sing-song voice, but nobody answered me.

"Hello?" I listened to somebody breathing heavily for a minute before I hung up. Almost as soon as I had put down the phone, it rang again. I picked it up but said nothing. I heard the same heavy breathing and slammed the phone down. It rang a third time, but I let the answering machine get it.

"I know you're there," the person on the other end whispered and hung up.

It was a low, creepy whisper. I played back the message several times, but I didn't recognize the voice. I thought it was a woman, but I couldn't be for sure. My machine recorded three more unsettling messages before I unplugged the phone. Damn. I'd been meaning to get caller ID for some time now. I fought the urge to call Gabriel. I didn't need him to run to my rescue. In fact, I didn't need him at all. And besides, it was probably just some kids fooling around.

When the doorbell rang, I jumped. I guess I was a little spooked. I slowly pulled back the curtain and peered at a young kid wearing a red jacket, holding a large square box. It was only the pizza delivery boy! I laughed at myself for being so startled.

The next night, the phone calls started at exactly seven o'clock.

"Who is this?" I asked, but received no response. "If you don't have anything to say, stop calling me," I demanded sternly.

Again, I unplugged the phone and made a note to call the phone company in the morning. I stared at the unplugged phone line in a daze, contemplating what to do, then I plugged it back in. It was *my* house and I wasn't about to let some prank caller disrupt my life. There, I thought, much better.

I was standing in front of the refrigerator with the door hanging wide open, searching for something to satiate me. I pushed aside the gallon of milk and peered over Saturday night's leftovers hoping anything would catch my attention. I stood there long enough for the milk to begin perspiring, but not long enough to find what I wanted. I closed the door, unsatisfied. What I craved wasn't in the refrigerator at all.

The instant the door slammed shut, the phone rang. My heartbeat accelerated as I picked it up. I didn't say a word and neither did the caller, at first. Then, cautiously, I heard, "Julia?"

Whew. It was Gabe.

"I'm here," I answered.

"You okay?"

"I'm fine," I said curtly.

"I tried to call several times last night and just a while ago, but it's been busy," he explained. "I was starting to worry. Are you sure everything's alright?"

"I unplugged the phone after a series of annoying hang ups." I didn't tell him about the heavy breathing or the creepy whispering.

"Who does that anymore?" he asked. "I thought prank calls were a thing of the past." Then he laughed. "Oh, that's right, my behind-the-times Julia doesn't even have caller ID."

He was right about that. Technology & I didn't get along well, so I avoided it as much as possible. Simple was better, I thought.

"Probably just some kids," I said.

"I was about to drive over and check on you."

"Thanks for your concern, Gabe, but I'm a big girl, so do me a favor and let me take care of myself." I was being a bitch, but I wanted him to see that I didn't need a man around.

"I don't know what the hell your problem is," he retaliated.

"You. You are my problem," I whined and hung up on him. Two seconds later, the phone rang.

"Gabe, this conversation is over," I blurted without saying hello.

"No Julia, it's not," the caller whispered. "Not until he's dead."

I dropped the phone and stepped back in shock.

"Mom!" Camden's scream sent me running into the family room.

"What's wrong?" I asked breathlessly.

"Blackjack pee'd on the carpet!" she tattled.

I breathed a sigh of relief. It was only dog pee. That, I could handle, but it would have to wait. I ran back to the kitchen and picked up the phone and punched in Gabe's number as fast as I could. The prank caller had gone too far.

Come on, Gabe. Pick up the phone. But he didn't answer, his voicemail did. After the recorded greeting and cue, I said in a shaky voice: "Gabriel, I need to talk to you. It's urgent. Please call me right away."

I called back again and left a second message and a third. Panic started to replace the air in my lungs. I didn't know what to do. Was Gabe in trouble or was I jumping to conclusions? Should I wait by the phone, hoping Gabe called back? I didn't want to waste precious time if, in fact, the call was a warning. And I couldn't just sit idle, waiting, wondering.

I grabbed my keys, yelled for Camden to put on her jacket and shoes and locked Blackjack in his crate.

"Where are we going, mommy?" Joey asked.

"To Grandpa's. Now hurry."

"Can we take Blackjack?" Joey would take the puppy everywhere if he could.

"No, we can't take Blackjack," I said as I hurriedly tied his shoes.

"Can we take Mr. Waddlesworth?" he asked, referring to a ratty stuffed duck he slept with every night.

"You are such a baby," Camden interjected.

"Camden, just get ready," I scolded. "Of course you can take Mr. Waddlesworth, honey," I said and zipped up his little blue jacket.

I peeled out of the driveway and headed straight to Gabriel's father's house.

"Julia, is something wrong? What's going on?" he asked, surprised to see me and the kids standing on his doorstep at eight o'clock on a school night.

"I'm not sure, Frank," I answered honestly and stepped inside. "But I really need you to keep the kids. I don't have anywhere else to take them."

Gabriel's parents had been divorced for years and his dad was living with a woman who used to teach English at Riverdale High. I felt disrespectful calling her by her first name instead of Mrs. McClimans, but she insisted that I call her Evelyn. She was coming down the stairs in her red silk pajamas. She was very well taken care of for her age and looked much younger than Gabe's dad, but they were great together and the children loved her. Joey even called her grandma.

"Julia, darling, come in and sit down," she insisted.

"Oh, I can't," I said anxiously. "I really hope I'm not interrupting anything."

"Don't be silly," she said. "I was reading the paper and this old fogy was falling asleep in his chair." She poked Frank in the side and winked at him.

"Where's Gabriel?" he asked.

"I don't know. I was actually hoping he'd be here."

"Here?" Evelyn looked surprised.

"Uh-oh. Trouble in Paradise?" Frank asked. "You look a little shook up."

"Shaken," Evelyn corrected him.

"Oh no," I lied. I muttered something about hearing a prowler at the house and wanting Gabe to check it out. I didn't want to worry him about the phone calls. He took medication for a heart condition and I didn't want to upset him.

"When will you be back, dear?" Evelyn asked.

"I'm not sure. I brought a bag for the children if it's late. Do you mind keeping them overnight if need be?"

"Never," she said smiling. "They are always welcome. Why don't you just come by tomorrow and get them before school."

"Are you sure?"

"Absolutely," she said.

"Thank you both." I kissed my children good night and told them I loved them to the moon and back. Then they rushed off to the kitchen for Frank's famous strawberry sundaes.

I shook my head in disapproval of the late snack, but they were excited and they were safe. *Yes Julia, the children are safe.* I had to reassure myself. My worst fear was that something would happen to one of them. They had been through enough in their little lives and although I had been selfish through some of that time, I loved them more than anything in the world. They were my life.

I replayed the last phone call in my mind as I drove over to Gabe's house. His car wasn't there, so I drove past the only bar he ever went to, but his car wasn't there either. Defeated, I went back home. My answering machine was full. Sixteen new messages.

Fifteen of them were noiseless. The last one was disturbing. It was the same voice.

"Not a creature was stirring, not even a mouse," was all the caller said. But this time, I could tell it was a female—it was a mature voice, like that of a woman. I was no longer dealing with some mischievous teenagers. I knew that much.

I argued with myself about what to do. *Call the police,* my inner voice told me. *Just call the police and let them handle this.* But no, I couldn't do that. What if it was nothing? Then I'd look like a fool. The police had more important things to deal with than a woman worried about her boyfriend. I frantically dialed Gabe's number again. And again, I was greeted by his voicemail. I was fighting the fear from rising up in my throat and I was trying to talk myself out of expecting the worst. I poured myself a glass of wine to settle my nerves. I gulped it down and poured another. I felt horrible for blowing up at him. But I had no time to dwell on that. I had to find him. *Think, Julia. Think!* If I were Gabe…

I knew Gabe better than anyone. I knew Gabe almost better than he knew himself. And suddenly, I knew where he must have gone. It made perfect sense. A woman scorned goes shopping. A man would do something that men do. When Gabe was upset, he sought solitude in fishing. That had to be where he went.

Gabe had a cabin in Pennsylvania. Well, it was more like a hunting camp. There was electricity and running water, but no telephone and no cell phone range. In fact, there was hardly any civilization at all.

The cabin itself was uncomfortably small, a bit shabby and full of spiders. But to Gabe, it was nirvana. I was certain that he left for camp right after our argument. The drive took nearly three hours, so I imagined he may be planning to get there, sleep, and be refreshed and ready to catch some fish early in the morning when he said fish bite the most. I couldn't bear the thought of him being there alone and in danger.

I had to go. There was no choice. I had to make sure Gabriel was safe. Despite his ignorance over the sanctity of marriage, I loved him. Admittedly, I had loved him all my life. Love. The strangest emotion of all. Happiness, sadness, safety, danger, birth, even death—all consequences of love. Sometimes it took more than it gave. Sometimes it devoured its prey.

I was a victim of love, but I couldn't imagine being anything else. Perhaps my greatest character flaw was loving too much and expecting the same love in return. My mother had taught me as a child that love is intangible, that it vanishes just as magically as it appears. Love leaves when you least expect it. Love leaves when you need it the most. And indeed, love may leave, but I'd never leave love. It held me captive, ensuring that I would love as long as I lived. And maybe that's the way it was meant to be. Love seemed to be a disease for which there is no cure. Once a loveaholic, always a loveaholic.

Enough philosophizing. I had to get to Gabe before anybody else did.

CHAPTER SEVENTEEN

G abriel, here I come. It was almost 10 p.m. I filled up the gas tank on my little black Toyota Camry and set off for the backwoods of Pennsylvania. Only I didn't make it there.

I already had a couple glasses of red wine before I got behind the wheel, but that was no big deal. It was only wine. I was extremely tired and beginning to feel foolish chasing after Gabe. I mean, what if the phone calls were just a joke? A sick joke, but still, a joke nonetheless. He would think I was checking up on him and he would have proof that what he said to me was true—that I was fragile and insecure. I couldn't let that happen.

I was more than halfway there and too uneasy to turn around, so I did what any vulnerable woman would do. I stopped at a roadside bar. Rusty Acres, I think it was called. It was shortly after midnight and the place was packed. Mostly locals, I presumed, by the stares I got when I walked in and sat on the only stool left at the bar. The jukebox was blaring country music so I had to shout to the bartender. A bottle of beer, I think that's what I started with. Then a guy wearing a cowboy hat asked me to play darts. Dang, he was hot. I obliged. After losing three straight games of Cricket, I sat back down and ordered some fries. I knew I should eat something before resuming my trip. So I ate and I drank. And I drank. And I drank. I wasn't keeping track. As soon as I'd finish one, another would be waiting for me, calling out to me. Just one more, they all said.

Finally, with my eyes irritated from the cloud of smoke that consumed the bar, I left. Rather, I lost my footing stepping off the stool and fell. The man who beat me at darts helped me up and I brushed myself off, rambling about some darn thing on the floor. I used the bathroom before stumbling out to the car. I had been staggering pretty badly, but I didn't think anyone noticed. I was fine, I told myself. I was just a little light headed from waiting so long to eat.

"Hey," I heard someone call out to me.

I turned around as I was opening my car door. It was the man with the cowboy hat.

"Are you okay?" he asked.

"Yeah, I'm good."

"Maybe you shouldn't drive just yet," he said.

Wow. In the dimly-lit parking lot, the cowboy was really good looking.

"What would you suggest instead?" I said in a flirty tone.

"Come back in and dance with me." He outstretched his hand toward me and smiled coyly. I only hesitated for a moment, then I put my hand in his and followed him back into the bar.

He selected a few songs on the jukebox and led me to the dance floor. I was lost in the music, leaning against him, concentrating on the words of the Travis Tritt song he had played.

"Even though you test my soul and make yourself so hard to hold, I'm gonna make you understand, I'm strong enough to be your man... And if you wonder if I'm strong enough to be your man ~ Yes, I am ~ Yes, I am..."

I tried to stop the tears from coming and from thinking about Gabriel. He shouldn't have been running away, he should've been running toward me. Was he really strong enough to be my man? Was anybody?

The cowboy lifted up my chin and our eyes met and locked. He wiped away a tear from the corner of my eye. Then he kissed me, slowly yet forcefully. I pulled back. I wasn't thinking clearly, I suppose, but I knew it was time to go. I walked toward the door while he quickly followed behind. I could hear his boots against the hardwood floor. I didn't turn around. I went straight to my car, intent on leaving this time.

He grabbed my hand as I fumbled to unlock my door.

"I'm taken," I said.

"I'm sorry. I didn't see a ring."

Slap. Right across the face. That's what it felt like. I stood there, stunned by his words. *That's right. You don't have a ring.*

Fuck you, Gabriel Jones. Fuck you for making me so distrustful, for promising to love me but for not understanding how important marriage is to me. Fuck you for not being strong enough to be my man.

I lurched forward and kissed him hard. He kissed me back. We never said another word to one another. With our lips locked, he rubbed his hands over my breasts. I should have stopped it. I should have remembered how angry and betrayed I was when Gabe had sex with Cara. I should have had some self-control. I should have had a damn ring on my finger. But I wasn't married, so what the hell.

He led me toward the back of the parking lot and he put down the tailgate of his Ford pickup truck. He took off his boots and jeans and I undressed quickly from the waist down. He lifted me up onto the truck and I wrapped my legs around him and laid back a little, giving him perfect leverage. Oh, it felt so good. It didn't last long. It was quick and hot. I was too old to feel dirty about it and too mad at Gabe to feel guilty. This would be my little secret.

I never asked him his name, he never asked me for mine. It was better that way. The mysterious cowboy from Pennsylvania was what I would always remember him as.

I was a little woozy walking to my car, probably a combination of the great sex and the alcohol, but I had to get back on the road.

*   *   *   *   *   *   *   *   *   *   *

The drive was quickly becoming tedious. It had been drizzling a little and the roads were a bit blacker than usual, so I put on my high beams and drove cautiously. Yawning, I turned up the radio. After that, your guess is as good as mine.

I think I may have closed my eyes, just maybe, just for a second. Then a warmth came over me like the two o'clock sun in July and a darkness set in—a quiet sanctuary I had never known. No windows, no shadows, no fear. Just dark. I wasn't alone, though. I felt someone tugging at me, someone shaking me, someone pulling me. Was it my father? No, it wasn't him. My grandpa? No, it wasn't him either. Was it a woman? Yes, I think it was. It was unfamiliar though. A whisper. Who was she? What did she want? Couldn't she see that I was content? I liked the solitude, the tranquility. I was finally at peace. *Just leave me be.*

But she didn't. She was pulling me, rather yanking me from the serenity. And it was hurting. Oh my God was it hurting. An unimaginable pain seared through my right arm. I thought maybe I was dead, but no, there could be no pain like this in death.

My foot was stuck on something, yet she tugged and tugged until it was finally dislodged. The pain was excruciating. It felt as if my foot were on fire. The burning pain brought tears to my eyes and they fluttered open for a split second, long enough to see the orangey-red glow of flames all around me. The heat was immense, but I was still shivering. I struggled to open my eyes again, but my head was too heavy to hold up and it lolled to the side.

I don't remember much after that. I don't recall hearing any other voices. There were no ambulance sirens, no flashing red and blue lights. Nothing seemed real. It was more like a twilight.

CHAPTER EIGHTEEN

Where was I? I was sitting upright on a bed, restrained and in dire pain. My ankles were tied together with what looked like heavy fisherman's rope. And so were my wrists. I was also tied across my lap with what I could only guess was a seatbelt and there was something holding my neck in place. I tried to open my mouth, but it felt as though the skin was being torn right off my lips. They had been taped shut. I was completely immobile and unable to speak.

There was an overpowering stench in the room. Maybe it was ammonia. Maybe cat urine. Perhaps there was a neglected litter pan nearby. Yeah, that's definitely what it smelled like.

I nervously glanced around the room, uneasy over its bare walls and strange arrangement of furniture. The bed was bolted to the wall opposite the door and there was a chair facing inward in each of the four corners of the room. My eyes shifted from chair to chair, disturbed at the prospect of their purpose. There was a small table at the foot of the bed with a disconcerting assortment of surgical instruments lined up on it, and a clock hung above the door. At least there was a clock. I squinted, trying to focus on the hands, but there were none. A clock without hands served absolutely no purpose except torment to someone who was as obsessed about the time as I was. "As useless as a man without a penis," Anna would've said. That was one of her favorite expressions.

And for God's sakes, why were there no windows? What the hell was going on? *Please God, please don't let me be part of some sick copycat of 'Misery.' I won't survive.* I fought to stay awake, to stay alert, but I drifted off and began dreaming of a beautiful, cascading waterfall. The colors were brilliant and vivid. I was floating through a garden of roses. Roses in every color—red, yellow, blue, purple, orange. I heard a dog barking from somewhere behind me and I turned around, expecting to see Blackjack. But this dog was much smaller and he was not at all black. Rather, he was green and speckled with yellow polka dots. The sun was only an arm's length away and I reveled in its warmth. The place was magical—far surpassing anything I could have ever imagined. Just then it started raining. Tiny drops of milk chocolate. I stuck out my tongue and caught them before they melted in my mouth. In the near distance, there was a majestic mountain slope congested with skiers anxiously waiting to board the lift. Despite the impeding sun and the chocolate rain showers, the mountain was covered with mounds of—no, not snow—coconut. Wow.

I was shaken back to my former state of semiconsciousness by her heavy footsteps. I yawned, stretching the tape at the corners of my mouth, ripping the skin further apart. My mouth was so dry, like a night after drinking too much cherry vermouth or bourbon.

I began to fade back into the haze again, but I felt her presence and it was unsettling. It took me a while to recognize her and when I did, I stared at her, confused and bewildered. She gazed at me callously.

"He said he loved you and only you. His precious Julia with your beautiful smile and your dainty fingers—fingers that were made to write for the God Almighty New York fucking Times," she said and paused, looking at me as though she were reflecting on what she had just said.

She gave me a strange, sick grin. *God help me. There is something so wrong here. I need help. I need Gabe.*

"He was so pathetically in love with you, but who the hell knows why. All you are is a spoiled little bitch."

I tried to control my breathing and keep myself from panicking. Had she already hurt Gabe? I couldn't bear the thought of losing him. I didn't want to provoke her, didn't want to rock her already-crazy cradle. I didn't struggle. I remained motionless. I just blinked, wide-eyed and silent—wide-eyed and scared.

I didn't like the way she was scrutinizing me. Didn't like it at all. She was picking up each and every one of my fingers, caressing them, staring at them as if they were a mouth-watering delicatessen that she was about to devour. Her eyes were transfixed and glassy, like she had been crying. She bent over and sadistically tightened the rope imprisoning my hands. My wrists burned insanely. *Please God, let it be fast. If she's going to kill me, let it be fast.*

She was humming as she worked on something that looked like a medieval torture device. *Oh God no. Please help me.* She kept humming like a sweet old grandmother does as she knits a blanket for her newly-born grandchild. My heart began to beat faster and faster. I looked away from her—I had to. I was losing my mind imagining what she could possibly have in store for me.

What the hell was she humming? It sounded so familiar, so freaking familiar. Then she stopped and marveled at her craftsmanship and began reciting a nursery rhyme in a disturbed, quiet voice, almost a whisper. *"All the king's horses and all the king's men couldn't put Humpty Dumpty together again."*

My eyes were wild with terror as she turned toward me. There was a lump in my throat the size of a golf ball. She slid a wooden table top over my lap—like the kind you eat on while in a hospital bed. Only this tray table had been fitted with corroded, rusty, ring-like metal bands—one for each finger.

"Put your hand in there," she demanded. But I resisted, clenching my fingers into a fist.

"I said put your fucking scrawny fingers in there," she ordered.

Her face was blank, completely expressionless. But she was determined to trap my fingers in her crude contraption. She grabbed my pinky on my left hand and bent it back as far as it would go before breaking. My fingers involuntarily loosened and she slammed my hand onto the wood slab, sliding my fingers under the metal rings. In one swift move, she clamped a thick metal bracelet over my wrist and snapped it into place, rendering my hand and all five fingers helpless. The clamp around my wrist was painful and tight, like a handcuff. The smaller clamps fell right above my knuckles and forced my fingers to be spread as far apart as they could go.

"Don't fight me, Julia. You'll only make things harder on yourself," she said wickedly. "Now put your other hand in here."

I struggled—my weakness against her maniacal strength, but my efforts were to no avail. Like my left one, my right hand was thrust into her barbaric device. And the wrist clamp was slammed down harshly, like a prison door being shut on a hardened criminal. But I had done nothing to be kept prisoner, I thought to myself. I had done nothing to this woman except be loved by the man she craved.

Now what? I thought. *"I'm sitting in the railway station, got a ticket for my destination, mmmhmm."* I closed my eyes, but only for a second. Homeward Bound. That was it. That was the song she was humming. Of all the songs in the world, she was humming that one. Why? *"I wish I was homeward bound. Home, where my thoughts escape me ~ home, where my music's playing ~ home, where my love lies waiting silently for me."* Oh I hoped my love was waiting for me.

She was crazy, that was for sure. Demented, mad, psychotic—whatever you want to call it. And most of all, she was dangerous. She had no compassion, no conscious. I could see it in her eyes. She stared straight into mine and laughed. A delirious laugh. A haunting laugh that seemed to echo from the shell of a person that she was.

I sat there stunned. She stopped abruptly and left the room, returning with a small bottle of what appeared to be nail polish. Yes, it was red nail polish.

"Oh beautiful Julia. If only Gabriel could see you now," she said smiling crazily. She sang as she dipped the tiny brush into the bottle and carefully polished each of my fingernails with the purposeful perfection of a manicurist.

"Wouldn't it be a shame," she said and paused thoughtfully, staring down at my hands. "If poor little Julia couldn't write anymore?"

There was that laugh. The high-pitched unstable laugh of a lunatic. Fear raced through me like a snake's venom entering my veins. What in God's name did she mean? She was warped beyond warped. The whole thing was so bizarre, so twisted. And there I was—a pawn in her devilish game and I was absolutely defenseless. I could no longer feel my legs. Paralyzed only by fear, I hoped.

I was silently whimpering and couldn't stop the floodgate of tears from rolling down my cheeks.

"You better stop that sissy crying," she snapped harshly at me. "Or I'll really give you something to cry about."

I was suddenly thrown back into my childhood. My mother had spoken those very words to me several times with just as much ruthlessness.

I blinked away the tears and watched her as she polished my final finger and set the bottle aside without closing it.

"There," she said. "We're almost ready." And she left the room.

Almost ready for what? I bucked back and forth violently, trying to free myself. I tried to scream for help, but the tape muffled my moans and kept my lips from opening. If I pulled my neck forward too far, the strap around it choked me. I was trapped. And my fate was in the hands of the most deranged woman I had ever known.

Cara didn't leave me alone for long. When she returned, she was holding a butcher knife. An old, dirty butcher knife with deep, reddish-brown stains in the wooden handle. *I am in real trouble here*, I thought. *What on Earth could that be for?* My breasts rose and fell, rose and fell, rose and fell as I begin to panic.

"My dearest Julia," she read aloud from a crinkled piece of paper. "Life is not worth living if I don't have you. You are all I ever wanted and all I've ever needed. You give breath to my existence," she read, her voice slightly wavering.

She was punishing me for words Gabriel must have written sometime before. Words I had never heard. If only I had never left Riverdale in the first place, there would never be any Cara in our lives. Of course there would also never have been Nick and Camden. I guess I couldn't dwell on the "if onlys." They would become a vicious cycle of could've, would've, should'ves and still, I'd be right where I was.

She continued reading the letter.

"All of my life I have waited for you and I'll continue to wait as long as I have to," she paused. "Aww, what a sweetheart," she said sarcastically. Then she went on. "I love everything about you. Every inch of your mind, every inch of your body—from your cute little nose to the tips of your fingers to the soles of your feet."

I sniffed and she looked up.

"God, I think I might puke," she said. "Have you heard enough, Julia? Have you?" she screamed.

All I could do was blink. I was so confused. Gabriel's letter was music to my ears—the only comfort in my hell. She was the one obviously devastated by his sincere devotion and proclamation of love for me—the other woman, in her eyes. She was torturing herself.

She slapped me across the face.

"I asked you a question," she said and once again began reading.

"Walking you down the aisle was the hardest thing I ever had to do, but making you my wife would be the best thing I could ever do." She was choking back her own tears.

"Oh, my love, marry me. Marry me and make me the happiest I can ever be. Marry me and love me until the end of time because," she paused, "that's as long as I'll love you."

Oh Gabriel, I thought. *Yes! Yes, I would have married you. It's what I've been asking you for, it's why I've been so angry and hurt.* But Gabe never wanted me to be his wife. If he did, he would have asked me. All Gabriel ever did was avoid marriage. Still, it sounded authentic. The letter sounded like my Gabriel Jones—the Gabriel Jones I knew my whole life, the Gabriel Jones who always loved me, the Gabriel Jones who unknowingly introduced a monster into our lives.

Cara waved the paper in front of my face. "You! You!" she shrieked. "It was always you and there was never any room for me. Well, you know what, you slut? I loved him, too. I loved him while you were whoring around in your big-shot city. You ruined my life and now you're going to pay!"

She held the knife firmly in her right hand, the way you do if you're going to chop an onion rather than slice it. Then, seeming as if in slow motion, she lifted it above her head and brought it down with perfect aim, right above the knuckle on my left ring finger—my wedding ring finger. The bottle of red nail polish spilled over; the red liquid gushed out.

Darkness. The pain was so intense, so agonizing, so indescribable. My eyes rolled back into my head in disbelief. No, more like utter shock. Anger. No, rage.

Pain. No, anguish. My mind was running the gamut of emotions.

My finger, what was left of it, went into a spasm, convulsing uncontrollably. Blood was flowing from the hideous stump. I had lost consciousness, but I was abruptly awakened when she dumped rubbing alcohol over my gaping wound. I felt like I was on fire. *Oh my God, the burning. Make it stop.* Not just my hand, but my whole body warmed instantly, then became cold and numb just as quickly as it had warmed. I was very confused. I didn't know if my finger was freezing or flaming. Just like uncovered ears in winter—they get so cold, they feel hot.

My senses were jumbled. My breathing was becoming slower and slower, almost still. And my ears were ringing intensely. I shut my eyes as tight as I could. I wanted to keep them closed forever, but seconds later they popped open. I watched her fiddling with what looked like a very thin string. Maybe it was thread. Maybe dental floss. I didn't know. I didn't want to know. She had wrapped gauze around my finger, but it was already blood-soaked and coming unraveled. She used the rest of the roll to cover her moment of insanity and roughly tied the string around it. It was extremely taut—like a tourniquet. I choked on my own vomit. Trapped inside my taped mouth, it had nowhere else to go but back down.

I heard music. Was it Paul? Was it Art? Yes, it was them. The rock and island song. *"A winter's day, in a deep and dark December, I am alone…"*

She was tormenting me with my favorite Simon & Garfunkel songs. Their words mirrored my own thoughts.

"I am shielded in my armor. Hiding in my room, safe within my womb, I touch no one and no one touches me..."

CHAPTER NINETEEN

Finally, a voice I recognized. I had no idea where I was or where I had been. I felt safe now though. He called to me, quietly, patiently waiting for a response. He called my name again. His voice was sweet and sincere.

"Julia." Then again, "Julia, it's me."

It was Gabe, but what was he doing here?

"Oh my sweet Julia, please wake up," he pleaded. "Please don't leave me."

He was sobbing. I was touched by his emotion but I *was* awake. He must be confused. *I'm right here, Gabe,* I said, but I didn't hear my voice. I spoke again.

Why would I leave you? I love you, Gabriel. My words were silent. *Oh my God, he can't hear me.* Then I started to panic. *He can't hear me. Why can't he hear me? Gabe! Gabe!* I yelled to no avail. Then the door opened and someone with soft-soled shoes walked in.

"Just doing rounds," she said. "How are you holding up?"

I'm not! I yelled in my mind. *Help me, please!* But she wasn't speaking to me.

"Not so good," Gabe said and sighed. "It's been three weeks." His voice sounded so forlorn, so despondent.

"Hang in there," the woman said. "She'll come around."

Wait a second. What was happening? Was I unconscious? Was I dreaming? I wasn't in a coma, was I? Oh my. It finally dawned on me. Then my mind blanked. I was panicking inside. I had watched a movie years ago—a true story—about a woman who had been in a catatonic state for seven years all the time hearing everything that had gone on around her.

Calm down, Julia. Calm down, I told myself. I just couldn't imagine it. I would go crazy listening for all that time unable to speak up, unable to wake up. I wouldn't last that long. My heart would just beat out of my chest and I'd go into cardiac arrest. *At least there's a way out,* I thought but I was still panicking.

"Wait, nurse!" Gabe yelled and she turned back on her heels. I was amazed at the sounds I could pick up. I was seeing with my ears, like a blind person.

"Her heart rate just went way up," he said optimistically.

The nurse must've been checking the monitor because she didn't say anything for what seemed like forever.

"Hmm," she answered puzzled. "She's probably just dreaming."

I'm not dreaming, you moron. I'm awake! I'm awake and I can hear you!

And I could hear her and Gabe and Anna, Frank and Evelyn and Camden and Joey. Oh, my precious babies. Joey's little plea saddened me.

"Please mommy, wake up," he said in his little boy voice. "I miss you."

I'm trying, baby. Mommy's trying.

And I heard all the nurses and the doctors.

"She's not in a coma," the doctor explained to my roomful of visitors. "She's in a deep unconscious state, but there is a chance that she can hear us. We've found that some unconscious patients can hear, understand and emotionally respond to the external environment, but because of their medical condition, they are incapable of communicating their awareness."

Yes, he's right! Yes, I can hear you! I can!

"This may sound foreign to you, but medically speaking, we know that the reticular activating system in the brainstem controls our ability to be awake, to sleep and to pay attention. This acts like a gatekeeper to consciousness, connecting with major nerves in the spinal column and brain. The mind can't function without these catalytic bundles and damage to them results in coma. Do you follow?" He asked like a teacher speaking to his students. They must've nodded in understanding because he continued.

"The damage to Julia's brain is very minimal. There are no severed nerves, no uncontrollable swelling of the brain. At this point, she may still be able to function at one-hundred percent. However, I have to be honest with you. If she doesn't arouse soon, she may slip into a deeper state of unconsciousness—a coma. With that, she may experience retrograde amnesia where she won't remember much before the accident."

I heard Anna gasp.

"There may also be loss of function both mentally and physically depending on the length of the coma and the severity of the brain injury," he said matter-of-factly.

"Doctor, what can we do?" Gabe asked.

"Just keep doing what you've been doing," he said. "Julia needs all the support she can get. Continue to talk to her, play her favorite music, touch her. Any stimulation that would hopefully evoke a response. I'll keep you updated on her status. In the meantime, we'll continue testing her and a physical therapist will see her regularly to keep her joints from stiffening. If you have any questions or concerns at all, please see any of the nursing staff and they will know where to find me."

Then he left. I had come to recognize his squeaky shoes. Gabe asked Anna if he could speak to her outside, which concerned me. What didn't they want me to hear? It seemed like forever that I was in my room alone, in complete silence. I wasn't asleep, though. At least my mind wasn't. It was running wild and scared.

Amnesia? Did they say I could forget everything if I

didn't wake up soon? Surely I could never forget Nick or my dad or Grandpa Joe. No way. All I had left of them were my memories. I had to wake up. Come on, Julia, wake up. Wake up!

The door opened and Anna sat down beside me. I was surprised that Anna had come. She talked to me as if we were having one of our infamous lunches at the Times Square Delicatessen. She missed those days, she said. She also told me that I had to wake up because I was the best friend she ever had. She cried and she blew her nose. She sniffled and then she cried some more. She said she was sorry over and over and over again.

Sorry for what? I thought. *Oh Anna, I'll be fine. Don't worry about me. Don't cry.*

She told me she was mad at me for looking so pretty in the hospital and she laughed.

"I know, Jules. Sickness is no excuse to look ugly," she said echoing what I had told her eons before when we worked at *The Times*. Those days seemed like they were a lifetime ago.

"In fact, why don't I polish your nails?"

No! Please don't even look at my hand! It must be so repulsive.

"I think I even have your favorite nail color in my purse. Yes, here it is. Red. Now won't that look nice? Of course it will. It'll look beautiful," she said.

I hadn't talked to her for months, but she was the same Anna, rambling on without taking a breath. She was trying to be helpful, but she was upsetting me. I didn't want my nails polished. I didn't want to draw any more attention to my disfigurement.

There are plenty of blanks. I'd hear someone say it was Monday and I'd fall asleep for a few hours, I thought, and a nurse would announce that it was Wednesday. It was scary and confusing and lonely. I had many visitors, that's not what I mean, but I wanted to reach out and touch my babies and Gabe. I was trapped within my own mind. It was maddening.

I don't know what I would have done without Gabe. He sat by my bed religiously. He talked to himself an awful lot, but mostly to me. He missed me, he said. And he regretted that he hadn't yet asked me to marry him. He wanted us to pay more attention to each other, to be able to finish each other's sentences like we used to. He said he brought me some music and he joked that he hoped his singing didn't put me into a deeper sleep. He played all the songs I loved like "I Am A Rock" and "Homeward Bound." I know the music I liked was much older than my generation, but I was drawn to the melancholy of their voices. A song was only worth listening to if you could feel the music. And I could feel Simon & Garfunkel. Gabe was the only one who knew that. He played "Bridge Over Troubled Water" at least a dozen times one afternoon.

"When you're weary, feeling small, when tears are in your eyes, I will dry them all," he sang along. *"I'm on your side, oh, when times get rough."* He sang softly and sweetly. *"Like a bridge over troubled water, I will lay me down."*

I was so touched. I wanted to hug him and tell him that he was the sweetest man in the world.

"I'll take your part, oh, when darkness comes and pain is all around." His singing was becoming interrupted by his crying.

"Sail on Silver girl, sail on by. Your time has come to shine. All your dreams are on their way... I'm sailing right behind."

Although he didn't know it at the time, Gabe and my children were the only reason I wanted to wake up, to free myself from the silence, from the darkness. If it weren't for them, I'd have let it swallow me — release me from the world that took so much from me, release me so that I may never be hurt again.

CHAPTER TWENTY

Six weeks after I was rescued, I opened my eyes. My vision was blurry, but I could actually see! It had been dark so long I wondered if I'd ever see again. I grimaced at the bright fluorescent light overhead. Squinting, I was starting to make out the shape of someone sleeping in the chair beside my bed. *Focus, Julia. Focus.* It was Gabe. My ever-so-loyal Gabriel Jones.

I tried to speak, to call out his name, but not even a whisper escaped from my lips. I was blinking uncontrollably and my eyes felt wet with tears. I stared at him until he awoke.

"Julia?" He asked in bewilderment and surprise. "Julia! Can you see me? Oh my God, nurse!" He yelled then pressed the buzzer to call the nurses' station. A nurse came running—I could hear her speeding down the hall.

"Hi, Julia," she said.

I concentrated on refocusing from Gabe to her. I recognized her voice, but just like imagining characters in a book, I pictured her shorter with blonde hair instead of red.

"Blink once if you can hear me," she said.

It was hard. I didn't want to close my eyes again, not even for a split second. But I did, as instructed. I think it was longer than a blink, but they were excited just the same.

"I've gotta call Anna and the kids!" Gabe said and he turned to leave, then quickly spun on his heels and kissed me on the cheek, then on the forehead and on the lips. Just little pecks, out of sheer jubilance. Boy, did I miss him. I didn't want him out of my sight. *No, Gabriel, don't go. Please don't go. Don't leave me. Don't you ever leave me. Come back! Come back and stay forever because that's as long as I'll stay. I won't ever leave again. I promise. Gabriel, I love you!*

I was told to get some rest, but how could I sleep? All I had done was sleep! I was anxious to see my children and to talk to Gabe. I had so many questions. No way was I falling asleep now, I thought, but my insubordination didn't last for long. I fought to keep my eyes open, but they were heavy and tired. The light only lasted another half an hour before the darkness swallowed it.

When I awoke, I was surrounded by all the people I loved. The nurse had taken the tube out of my throat and although it was incredibly sore and dry, I was able to manage a whisper.

"I love you," I said. "I love all of you."

And then, with courage I had mustered from their strength, I looked down at my left hand. I was in absolute shock. I closed my eyes for a second and pinched myself, wondering if I was still dreaming. It was no dream. My left hand looked much different than the last time I had seen it. Tears streamed down my face and I turned to Gabriel. I didn't know what to say.

On my finger, the finger I thought was no longer there, was the most beautiful ring. A diamond ring. An engagement ring.

My memory was cloudy so Gabe filled me in on what had happened. He explained that I had been in a terrible accident in Pennsylvania on the way to his cabin. A woman pulled me from the wreckage moments before my car was engulfed in flames and drove me to the hospital herself. She had told him she didn't want to leave me on the side of the road to go call for help. It took a while to sink in. I had gone straight from my car to the hospital. *What? How could that be? What about Cara?* Gabe answered me as if he was reading my thoughts. Apparently when Cara heard about my accident, she called Gabe and confessed that a friend of hers had been making those frightening phone calls to me on her behalf. She told him she felt childish and guilty and asked if she could come and apologize in person. She said she never meant any harm. Ah, so she had been in my room, but she didn't come to hurt me. There was no chamber of horror. There was no vengeful torture. It had merely been a figment of my imagination.

Tragedy incites passion. Gabe and I vowed to throw caution to the wind and give in to love. Life wasn't perfect. It never would be. In our most memorable, most heartfelt conversation, Grandpa Joe had warned me against expecting perfection.

"Darling, only fools look at life through rose-colored glasses," he had said. And I shook my head in understanding, agreeing that I wouldn't fall prey to life's little misconceptions. And I didn't. No, instead I had been looking at life through amber-colored shades. All that I ever needed or wanted had been standing before me and I was too foolish to see it.

What a voracious appetite for destruction love has. How much of life I had wasted searching for that elusive love when all along I had the greatest love in the world. A love so pure, so simple, so real. But fate is a bit forgetful and not always kind. Someone once told me to love deeply and passionately. And even though you may get hurt, it's the only way to live life completely. Great love involves great risk. I now understood that. And I would do my best to remember that without love, I had nothing.

Gabriel Jones had always been the most important one in my life — if only I had seen it before. Before all the heartache, before all the tears, before all those years had passed us by. How different it all could have been — like maybe if I had zigged instead of zagged. If only I had read the last page first.

Paul & Art's words echoed from years before: *"All my words come back to me, in shades of mediocrity... like emptiness and harmony, I need someone to comfort me."*

Reflecting on what I had come to learn, I went to the one place I could always find solitude. A place of utter stillness. A place of ultimate serenity. A place where I could talk to him for hours, and although I knew he wasn't there, I somehow always felt that he could hear me. And if I listened real hard, I could almost hear him talk back to me.

The cemetery. That's where I went. I visited the spot where Grandpa Joe had been finally laid to rest.

"Life didn't turn out all that bad after all, Grandpa," I spoke aloud to the gray tombstone that memorialized my dear old grandfather.

"No, Julia," I imagined him saying. "It sure ain't plum puddin', but it ain't nothin' to give up on."

His final words of wisdom from our final conversation suddenly came rushing back to me.

"We're bound to go astray, Julia, but eventually we all find our way home."

Home. I was home, once again, and home was where I'd stay. I looked up at the ominous clouds and said goodbye to Grandpa Joe, to my father, to Nick. And I closed my eyes in remembrance, but only for a moment. It was time to open them, to see more clearly, to abandon my cynical views and to finally, stop looking at life through amber shades.

ABOUT THE AUTHOR

Amber Shades is the first novel author *Laura Leigh Leskovac* has written. Writing has been a passion of hers since early childhood. She first penned this story when she was 24 years old, but the manuscript stayed hidden in a manila envelope for 12 years before she brought it to life thanks to a friend who simply asked to read her story. *Laura Leigh Leskovac* is a wife and mother of three children. She describes herself as an "every day, ordinary mom" who juggles her career with her family, with whom she most enjoys spending her time. She also has a passion for her hometown community of Greenville where she is a relentless supporter and an avid volunteer. *Laura Leigh Leskovac* credits her mastery of written language to the wonderful English teachers she had along the way.

Made in the USA
Lexington, KY
29 July 2014